ALLURE

PAGETURNER
PRESS&MEDIA

BY

GINA FERGUSON

Printed in the United States of America

ISBN:	Softcover	978-1-63871-829-1
	eBook	978-1-63871-830-7

Republished by: PageTurner Press and Media LLC
Publication Date: 01/03/2022

To order copies of this book, contact:
PageTurner Press and Media
Phone: 1-888-447-9651
info@pageturner.us
www.pageturner.us

My name is Darby Daxton Deel, I am the sole proprietor of the Bare Day Spa in Big Bay Lake. Today starts off light and ordinary, until I reach my desk at work; the stack of bills and repair tickets that line my desk are evidence that the business hasn't been profitable in all most a year. I sigh with disappointment and continue looking at the bills; I can feel the tears of my reoccurring anxiety flaring up, as I fumble through the financial craziness on my desk.

My cousin Rachel Everly is a financial investor for Rico Investments; she has been working very diligently on a deal to partner my business with Park-Slate Industries. Unfortunately, the very handsome CEO Brett Slade is playing hard to get and frustrating us with his games. *How hard is it to find someone to partner with? I wonder. The location is perfect, a stones' throw from the hotel at Big Bay Lake and accessible parking too.* The phone rings, startling me back to reality.

"The Bare Day Spa." I chirp. "Darby speaking." "How may I help you?"

"Hello Darby." She sounds happy. "It's Rachel."

"Good morning, Rachel." My heart beats a little faster. "What's up?"

"I have good news." Rachel sighs. "And a little bad news too."

"Okay go with the good, first." I chuckle. "Then…"

"Darby." She releases an agitated sigh. "Mr. Slade has agreed to partner with you."

I feel a big but… Holding my breath. “Yes.” Then, I sense a positive vibe from Rachel.

“But…it isn’t impossible.” She adds.

“Go on.” Taking a deep breath. “I am listening.”

“He wants to meet with you.” Rachel utters quickly. “To discuss how you run your business.” “And then he wants to.” She gives a long pause and I exhale a little terrified. “Rename the business too.”

“Okay.” “But.” I reply sadly. “Why rename it?”

“Mr. Slade.” Rachel ignores my question. “Will be there today.” She announces. “Around four o’clock.”

“Rachel.” I retort. “Are you going to be here too?”

“I’ll be there.” She sighs.” “Only for the contract signing.”

“What?” I spat upset. “Why?” “Aren’t you my back up?”

“Yes.” “Unfortunately, cousin.” “I am not allowed to be at your meeting.” Rachel speaks sternly. “Per Mr. Slade’s request.”

“Oh-h.” *I can feel my face flush with desire. I’ll be alone with him. “As he requests.” I’ve only seen pictures of him, he is a fiercely good-looking man.*

“Darby.” “Darby.” Rachel charges knowing exactly what I am thinking. “Hey!” “Snap out of it.” Unfortunately, my luck in love has been sad to say, but I am a hopeful romantic.

“Sorry, Rachel.” I sigh deeply. “I was thinking about…”

“Tomorrow.” “You.” “And.” I can feel her smirking on the other side of the phone line. “Mr. Slade.” “He is gorgeous.”

“Yes…he is.” I still can feel my face blushing.

“Don’t worry.” Rachel giggles. “I’ll be a phone call away.”

“Okay…” I add. “Are you coming for lunch today?”

“No.” “I have to write up the contracts.” Her voice turns

sympathetic. "Have legal check them out." "And send one over to Mr. Slade's office." She utters. "But I will call you later."

"Thanks Rachel." I garble. "I'll talk to you later." "Bye."

"Bye, Darby."

I place the phone receiver back on its base and go back to clearing off my desk in preparation for todays' business. My first client for the day is due any moment, he is new to the spa, so I rush into the first room and make sure that it is set for him. The massage table has the sheets and towels ready, the oils are set, and the stones are heating up in a water bath and I hear the door chime upon returning to my desk. The gentleman is middle-aged gray-haired, tall with a moderate build, a sweet smile and very good looking for his age.

"Good morning, Sir." I smile. "Please sign in." "This is your first visit at Bare Day?"

"Yes, Ma'am." He nods. I get a whiff of his fiery cologne, its vibrant and alluring.

"Darby, please." I smile and stutter a little. "I need a copy of your driver's license." I spill. "And you'll need to fill out some paper work too."

"Thank you, Darby." He sooths. "My name is Will." "Here is my license."

"Thank you, Will." I take his ID. "And here is your paperwork."

Will smiles brilliantly, sits down in a chair against the wall facing the desk and in full view of me; he begins filling out the papers as I type in Will's information from his driver's license in the computer.

"M-mm, his last name is Slade." I mumble loudly. "I wonder if he is related to Brett Slade."

"Yes, I am." He speaks up, starling me. "Sorry. I didn't mean to scare you." "He's my brother."

"Oh, I didn't mean to…" Saying embarrassingly.

"No, no its okay." "I get it." His voice calms. "The last name strikes you."

"I wasn't trying to imply anything." I smile making eye contact. "He is supposed to be my business partner soon."

"Oh yeah." His forehead wrinkles in thought. "That makes sense…why I am here." Will bellows. "Brett can't do his own dirty work."

"What?" I glare unsure of what I heard. "I don't understand." "Dirty work?"

"Sorry, I wasn't meaning you." His voice stammers. "He's always passing things along to me, without asking." Engagingly stares. "It's okay." "Miss Deel." He jokes. "I am a paying customer for the first hour." "I expect a great massage." *I wonder what he's up to. He's not who he seems.*

"You'll get one." "But…" My lips tremble with a tint of anger. "Finish the paperwork first, Mr. Slade."

"Yes, Ma'am." He smiles. "Back to paperwork." "And." "Please… call me Will."

"Sure." I smile unsettlingly. "Will." "You have five minutes before we get started."

"Okay." "Darby." A few moments later, he hands me the clipboard. "I'm finished."

"Thank you, Will." I breath deep. "Please go into room one, undress, lay down on your stomach on the table and cover yourself with the sheet waist down." "And I'll be in shortly." I smile. "Oh, hangers are on the back of the door for your clothes."

"Thank you, Darby." He waltzes into the massage room.

As I review Will's paperwork; I notice he is on several medications, including an anti-anxiety. *Mm-m weird. That could explain a lot. I laugh internally.* I finish at the computer and head to the massage room. Will is lying flat on his stomach on the table, the sheet is draping across his mid-section when I walk inside the room.

"Will." "Are you comfortable?"

"Yes." "I am a little." He says nervous. "It's drafty in here."

"Oh." "No worries." I assure him. "Once the massage starts, you'll warm up."

"Ok." "What's first?"

"I am going to place hot stones on your back." "I'll be placing them on pressure points." I say sensually. "It will help you relax."

"Oh." He moans. "Sounds nice."

"Let me know if they cause any discomfort." I smile. "Here we go." I place the five stones strategically down his spine. Will sighs. "Now I'll return in a few minutes to begin the massage."

"Oh." Will mumbles. "This feels good." "Yes, I'll be waiting."

I place the cold bottle of oil in the hot water bath to warm it and leave the room. I return to my desk and the phone rings. The caller ID shows Park-Slate Corporation is calling, my stomach tightens, and I grab the receiver quickly.

"Hello." "Bare Day Spa." I rush out. "Darby speaking." "May I help you?"

"Hi Darby." "My name is Marilee." She uncaringly utters. "I am Mr. Slate's secretary."

"How can I help you Marilee?"

“Mr. Slate would like to meet you.” She clears her throat. “In an hour.”

“I thought he was coming by.” I say unnerved. “Around four this afternoon.”

“Yes.” “But his meeting was cancelled this morning.” Her voice simmers. “He would like to see you sooner.”

“Well, I have a few clients this morning.” I breathe. “Would he mind if I call him back after my appointments are complete?”

“Please hold and I’ll confer with him.” The moment of silence seems long. “Darby.” “Mr. Slade is okay with you calling him back.” “But he wants you to call him on his personal cellphone.”

“Oh.” “Okay.” My mind rushes. “Let me grab a pen.” “Marilee, I am ready.” I jot the number down quickly. “Thank you.” “I’ll call as soon as my last client is done.”

“Thank you.” Her voice calms me slightly. “Darby.” “Have a nice day.”

“You too.”

Hanging up the phone, I stand dumbfounded for a second; then return to finish Will’s massage. Will has fallen asleep and he is snoring. I laugh quietly. I slowly remove the stones, not to wake him, take the oil bottle out of the water bath and place the stones back in the water. I pour some oil on my hands, starting with his shoulders and neck; Will begins to stir and smiles.

“I fell asleep.” He slurs. “Didn’t I?”

“Yes, you did.” I giggle. “With a soft snoring serenade.”

“Oh no.” He mumbles out. “I am so embarrassed.”

"No need." "Relaxation is important." I announce. "Plus, it helps with the massaging."

"Okay." He lays totally relaxed. "I'll lie here." "And enjoy." I finish Will's posterior side, he flips over slowly on the table; his face is reddening because he has an erection. "I am beyond embarrassed." He covers his face with his hands. "I don't know what to do."

"Well, this is unfortunate." I declare trying not to smile. "But it is a normal reaction to a massage for some men." "Are you currently on any medications for ED?"

"Yes." He blurbs. "But I didn't list it on the form." "Sorry."

"No problem, Will." "I know certain pressure points to resolve this issue." "May I?"

"Yes, please." I slide my hand across his inner thigh, apply pressure in his groin area and his erection drops down; he touches my hand gently and smiles. "Thank you." I note there is something sexual in his touch, but I dismiss it.

A few minutes later, I complete Will's massage and I leave the room; he dresses, stops to pay at my desk and schedules another massage. Will makes an appointment for next week at the same time as today. The next three clients arrive on time, and I complete their massages. My hand shakes as I dial Mr. Slade's number and it rings twice.

"Hello." "This is Slade." His voice plays. "Hello."

"Oh." "I am sorry." I fumble. "Hi." "This is Darby from Bare Day Spa."

"Oh, yes." "Ms. Deel." He says business like. "I am ready to tour your facility." "May I stop by in twenty minutes?"

"Yes." "You can come now." My heart races. "If you'd like."

"Ms. Deel." He rattles controllingly. "I'll…be there in twenty minutes." *He's rude, like a stiff suit.*

"Okay, see you soon."

The phone disconnects abruptly, and I place it back on the cradle. I survey each massage room for cleanliness and to restock supplies; then I walk into my office to fix my hair and makeup. Meanwhile, Mr. Slade arrives early letting himself inside, views the waiting area and desk; he hears a woman's sarcastic voice muttering from inside the office and he goes over to check it out. In the mirror, I am speaking with a winey voice, repeating Mr. Slade's exact words. *Ms. Deel. I'll be there in twenty minutes. How rude? Like his time is more important than mine.* He smiles, deliberately clears his throat in my office door way and my stomach tightens; I turn, facing the most handsome man I'd ever seen and he's smiling; losing my balance a little, I fall back into the mirror and brace myself.

"Ms. Deel." "I presume." He says smugly. "My name is Brett Slade."

"Hello." "Mr. Slade." I counter slyly. "Please call me Darby."

"Dar…by." He makes eye contact and sensually smiles. "Please call me Brett." I nod. "Okay let's get on with the tour." He commandingly waves his hand. "If you'd please."

As Brett and I walk through the massage rooms, tanning bed area, manicure and pedicure area; I can feel his eyes surveying my frame, I sense a sexual connection between us. I continue explaining how my

Spa works closely with the Big Bay Hotel; they refer clients to the Spa and I to the hotel. Rolling on, I express my desire to add a hair salon; so that it would be complete head to toe Spa, where both sexes can relax, taking a day away from the craziness of everyday life. Brett's facial expressions start to show interest in my dreams, even though his body language suggests something else. We return to my office, I sit at my desk, Brett sits in one of the chairs in front of my desk and stares at me; while sliding his left hand into his slacks pocket next to his manhood, purposely making sure I notice. *And I do*. I feel the heat of desire crawling up my sultry legs, my heart beats faster.

"Well, Brett." My face flushes with the heat of the moment. "What do you think?" I feel confident. "Can we be partners?" My core softly pulsates, he shifts his weight in the chair and removes his hand from his pocket to his lap, and smiles.

"Darby." His eyes twinkle at me. "Honestly." My hands tighten on the arms of my chair. "You are doing well on your own." "But I think the real problem is advertising." He shrills. "Publicity." "Nobody knows you're here." He is back to business.

"Okay." "I am a little confused." I stare at him. "Are you going to help me?" "Or partner with me?"

"Both." "I think we can make this Spa…universal." He's excited. "With the right promotion." "You." His eyes soften with a brilliant smile. "We could become very successful." Once again, I feel tingles of desire ebbing my brain

"Shall I call Rachel for the contracts?" I say intently. "Or you?"

"No." "I'll call." He stands, again sliding his left hand into a pocket of his slack near his maleness, I quickly look away to avoid staring, then I watch intently waiting for him to leave my office. "She will need to change a few items in the contract." Brett smiles enjoying his toying with me. "I'll call you later."

"Hey, I am starving." I smile sensually trying to keep him here. "Why don't you join me at the Big Bay Hotel for dinner?" I know Brett feels our attraction, but something is off.

"Yes, I would like to." "But." He frowns with a sigh. "I need to take care of some business back at the office first." "How about if I meet you at the restaurant around six?"

"Okay." Smiling. "I'll go home and change." "And meet you at six."

"Casual or formal?" His eyes reply with desire.

"Casual." I insinuate seductively. "Unless…"

"Darby, it is only dinner." His lips spout quickly.

Only dinner. U-huh... But the slight bulge in his slacks suggests differently and my desire swells. He walks out of my office quickly.

I turn off lights, shut down the computer, fasten the front door and head to my car for the drive home; Brett is waiting outside the limo, he watches me get into my car, then he gets inside the black limo waiting for him. The drive home is not long but picking out a dress for dinner is going to be a challenge. My house is a quaint medium size cottage with a two-car garage and a large backyard. I enter my dwelling going directly to my bedroom and head quickly into my closet, which has an assortment of different styles of dresses, pant suits and skirts; I stare at them and scream. *"I need Rachel."* Grabbing the phone off its receiver, I dial Rachel's number; it rings four times before her voicemail comes on, I leave a desperate message pleading for help as soon as possible.

I return to my closet and continue searching for the perfect outfit. Finally, a few minutes later I find three outfits I like, but I can't decide on one. The phone rings, it's Rachel; she agrees to help and drives to my house a few minutes later.

"Hey Rachel." I sputter. "Get in here quick." I grab her arm as I open the front door. "I need you."

"Don't be so rough." She asks. "I am going." We go to my closet and I show her the outfits.

"What do you think?"

"Neither one." "Let me look." She pushes the hanging clothes. "Here it is." "Darby." Rachel dances. "This is perfect." "Try it on." She picks a beautiful light gray cocktail dress with a beaded neck line.

"Are you sure it is not too dressy?" Rachel shakes her head no. "Your right." I gasp. "I am meeting…Brett Slade for dinner." I feel like a nervous teenager on her first real date.

"Yes, you are." Rachel says. "He's the most eligible man in town." "And he agreed to meet you for dinner." She sounds like a giddy teenager too.

"I know." "It is so exciting." I notice a little jealousy in Rachel's tone. "But, Brett will be my business partner soon." Rachel totally ignores my comment.

"Oh, yeah." "The new contract will be ready tomorrow." Rachel expresses. "I'll meet you and Mr. Slade at the Spa around noon."

"Did you let him know?" I ask. "If not, I can tell him at dinner."

"Yes, I tried." "But his phone went to voicemail." Rachel rattles "If you would, let him know." I step out of the bathroom and Rachel smiles big. "You look beautiful, Darby."

"Thank you, Rachel." I hug Rachel. "It's almost six." "I've got to get going." "Lock the door when you leave."

"Okay, I'll clean up in here." Rachel utters as I rush out of my bedroom. "Get out of here." "Don't keep him waiting."

I walk quickly out of my house, get into my car and drive to the Hotel. I had forgotten how beautiful the restaurant lobby looks with its huge gold and crystal chandelier; every time I enter, its magic reminds me of an old mystical castle. The distinguished Mr. Brett Slade is standing next to the concierge desk waiting; he smiles handsomely when his eyes meet mine, my legs wobble a little as he walks towards me; his hand softly touches mine as he lifts it to his warm lips to kiss and smiles brilliantly, the attraction between us is undeniable.

"Darby." "You look amazing." He sighs. "Let's go…to the dining room."

"Thank you." I sensually unravel. "Mr. Slade."

"Please." He sultry mumbles. "Call…me, Brett."

"Okay." I breathe sensually. "Brett." He takes my hand to lead the way; his touch sends tingles throughout my body. "Let's…go."

The Maître d' walks us to the table; it faces the windows overlooking the historical gardens of Big Bay Lake. We get comfortable at the table, the Maître d' places the napkins in our laps and hands us menus; Brett's hand stretches across the table, he takes mine hand softly and smiles.

"Shall I order for us." "Or would you like to…"

"Oh-h." I sigh, while my knees shimmy with desire. "Please do."

"Are you okay?" He smirks with interest. "You look..."

"I assure you, I am fine." My heart is fluttering. "The view is beautiful."

"Yes…she is." He sees through me, I blush. "And the gardens are gorgeous too."

Dinner is delicious, the company is divine, but what happens next is a total surprise to me. Brett asks me to dance with him in the ballroom; one dance turns to two and then until midnight, he's electric, passionate and I am completely fascinated with him. Brett offers to drive me home in my car, I accept. We leave the Hotel, he is a gentleman and opens the passenger door for me; as our fingers touch it sparks fiery magic as he holds my hand when I take my seat inside the car; the heat between us is growing. When we arrive at my house, my heart races and I feel nervous; he opens the door, walks around the outside of the car to my door and opens it. Brett reaches for my hand, I give it to him and he helps me outside the car; his arms wrap around my waist, he pushes me back against the open door shutting it behind me and he smiles.

"May I kiss you?" He breaths. "Darby."

"Yes." His first kiss feels warm, tingly on mine.

The second one is electric with desire, and I kiss him back with passion; quickly his arms release me, he coldly walks me to my door and my body still quivering with excitement. Suddenly, Brett seems weird and indifferent. *Why?* We reach the front door, he kisses the top of my hand, instead of my lips. I stare in doubt.

"Goodnight, Darby." He says cold. "I'll see you Tomorrow."

"Brett." "What's wrong?" I'm dumbfounded. "You kissed me." "And…"

"You kissed me back." Brett clears his throat backing away. "We can't…" "We are going to be business partners."

"I know that." I'm mystified. "But you feel it too."

"Yes, but…" He breaths and launch into him. "We…" I stop him with a kiss. "Darby."

"Brett, come inside." I say sensually. "Stay." "I want you too." I sigh, and he smiles.

"Not tonight, Darby." He utters. "I can't."

"Okay, Brett." The tears began to form, but I didn't let him see. "See you Tomorrow."

I close the door behind me. Brett calls his driver, but I didn't hear him leave right away, looking outside a few minutes later and he is gone. The heat of the water in my shower couldn't compare to the fire he ignited inside me; the hot water cascades down my body and I imagine it is his fingers touching me and until my core spasms with release. I feel alone, but the exhaustion of the day takes over and I crawl into bed, falling fast asleep.

My dreaming starts with an exceptionally crazy client, her requests are unusual, but they turn out with amazingly great results. Then, I am sitting at my desk in the Bare Day Salon feeling alone and deprived. When Brett walks in the office, he sits in the chair in front of me for the contract signing; his sexy smile entices me to suspect there is an additional requirement in our contract, sex. I stand up and walk around my desk to sit on his lap facing him; our lips touch and I wake up from my dream, sweaty and wanting him. Brett is obviously tempting me, I stumble out of bed and into the kitchen to make coffee. I notice a dozen red roses in a vase on the counter. At first thought, how did he get inside my house, feeling invaded and scared. The fear goes away when I see the note; it reads: "Darby, I am sorry about last night. Thank you for a wonderful evening. Brett." What should I think or feel? Is he interested or not? Was it a dream? The roses are beautiful, and they smell wonderful. I start the coffee pot, go back to my bedroom to get ready for work, make a quick breakfast, drink coffee and grab my purse to leave for work; I open the front door, Brett's limo is waiting outside, he steps outside the vehicle smiling and waves me forward to him.

"Brett, what is it?" I ask standing in front of him. "Why are you here?"

"I thought that I'd drive us to work today." He opens the door. "Please get in."

"I can drive myself to work." I stare inquiring. "Why are you really here?"

"Darby, please get in." His face is stern. "I want to talk to you."

"We can talk at the salon." I speak declaring strength. "I'll meet you there." I walk away and get into my car. Brett quickly climbs into my car, sitting in the passenger seat next to me. "What are you doing?"

"Well, you won't let me take you to the salon." His face is blank. "I want to say…" He pulls me to him. "I-I am sorry." His lips touch mine and sparks fly.

"What are you doing?" I push away. "Last night, you made it clear." "We are in business together." "And..." His arms pull me in quickly, this time his kiss surges in deeper, igniting my fiery core and I want more. "Darby, do you have clients scheduled this morning?" Brett breaths.

"Yes." I sigh passionately.

"Let's go." He backs off and declares untidy. "To the salon." *What the hell, is he into me or not? He's so confusing.*

My hands shake a little starting my car and we leave for the salon. As I unlock the door to the salon, his hand brushes mine and it send tingles to my most intimate place. We walk inside, I turn on lights, switch the computer on and walk into my office. Brett is close behind me, I can feel his intense stare; he places his hand on my lower back and I turn to face him. My mind is in a panic, but my lips want to kiss his undeniably.

"Can I help you?" His eyes shimmer. "I can make coffee." His hand on my lower back begins to slide lower.

"Sure." My heart is racing. "Let-me-show you where everything is." I clear my throat and his eyes release me. "Then…I can show you how to set up a massage room, too."

"Sounds great." Brett asks curiously. "Maybe, you can teach me how to do a massage?" Taking a step closer to my body.

"Yes, good idea." I move slowly past him, inadvertently brushing my hand across his crotch. "Follow me." I smile blushing.

I show him around the little kitchen and he starts the coffee pot. The door chime goes off, my first client is here, and I rush to the front desk. The older lady has a painful look on her face, she tries to smile signing in, while Brett admires me from the doorway of the kitchen.

> "Nancy." I ask with concern. "Are you okay?" "What happened?"
>
> "Oh, Darby." She utters in pain. "George asked me to help him in the garden yesterday." Air rushes out of her mouth, Nancy places her hand on her chest, face goes pale and sweaty. "And I think I did too much."
>
> "Okay." I smile sweetly. "Well, let's see if I can relieve some of that tension and pain." "Go to room one." Nancy slowly walks over to room one. "Nancy if you need help, give me a shout."
>
> "Okay, Darby." She breaths heavy. "You're a sweetheart." Nancy disappears into room one and I pick up the phone to call George at home.
>
> "George, this is Darby at the salon." Spouting serious concern. "I think Nancy maybe having a heart attack." I announce. "I am calling EMS to standby if I need them." Brett is amazed, his heart races as his watches me in action.
>
> "I'll be there, shortly." George pleads over the phone line. "You take good care of my girl."
>
> "I'll do my best, George." My hands shaking a little. "Be careful driving." "Bye." I take a deep breath and dial 911. "Hello, this Darby from the Bare Day Salon." "I want you to come to the salon." Stating clearly. "I think one of my clients maybe having cardiac issues." "Please don't run the siren." "It may upset her more." "Hurry, thank you."

Brett launches from the doorway and catches me from behind, when I start to fall back off balance; I smile in his arms and his eyes twinkle, he releases me, and I walk into room one. Nancy is halfway on the table, clutching her chest and I yell.

"I need help, Brett." "Now!" He rushes into the room. "Help get her on the table." We lift her together on to the table and cover her with the sheet. "Nancy, I have help coming." "Slow deep breaths." Brett is standing stiff and pale. "Brett." "Brett." He looks at me and nods. "You need to go let the paramedics in." "Nancy, slow deep breaths." The ambulance arrive as Brett swings the front door open.

"Hey Mr. Slade, where is the patient?" Brett points to room one. "Thank you."

The paramedics rush into room one with a gurney in tow. I walk out to the lobby, Brett sitting on the stoop outside and he has tears in his eyes. I rush to his side and hold him close. George arrives while the paramedics are wheeling Nancy outside to the ambulance; he talks to the paramedics and follows the ambulance to the hospital. I kiss Brett's cheek and continue holding him close. He lifts his head, smiles and kisses me softly on the lips. I realize that I 've seen the sensitive, caring man underneath the tough untouchable rude businessman.

"Thank you, Darby." Brett sniffs.

"Are you okay?" I stare at him. "Why are you crying?" "Did you know Nancy?"

"No." He stammers. "But, it stirred up memories of my mother before she died."

"You still miss her." I smile. "Aww, that's so sweet."

"Darby." "You are an amazing woman." Brett raves. "Keeping your cool, in an emergency."

"You wouldn't say that, if you knew how much I am shaking inside." Replying in quivering voice. "Let's go inside." "I need to check my schedule." As I get to my feet, I fall into him, his lips brush mine and we kiss. "For someone, who is all business." I whisper. "You sure know how to kiss…me."

"The contract hasn't been signed yet." He moans and kisses me again with more desire.

"What does that mean?" I shove him away upset. "Once we are partners…this is over." "Whatever this is?"

"Yes, I guess…it does." Brett sneers. "I never mix business with pleasure." Suddenly, I feel nauseous.

"You're a bastard." I hammer. "I'll call Rachel and we can be business partners." I grit my teeth. "Only business partners." "That's fine with me."

"No, I'll call her." He smirks, like he is laughing at me. "And the jury is out on us."

"There is no us." I whisper to myself walking inside the salon to my office. "Never-ever." The next two client visits seem quick and easy, but it feels like time stops between us. A few minutes after sitting in my office, the phone rings and it is Rachel.

"Darby." She asks. "Is Mr. Slade at the salon?"

"Yes, I think so." "Hold on." I place the phone receiver on my desk and step to the doorway.

"Brett." I announce outside the office doorway. "Rachel is on the phone."

"Okay, Ms. Deel." His voice is cool. "Thank you." "I'll take at the front desk."

"Your welcome, Mr. Slade." I reply aloofly and transfer the call. The call took all of five minutes and it ended. Brett stands in my doorway and smiles.

"Ms. Deel, we are meeting Rachel at the Big Bay Hotel for lunch in an hour." His words sound commanding. "Is that suitable for you?"

"Yes." "Your car or mine?" I state sternly. "Or separately?"

"We can ride together, if you like." Brett lips straight.

"That's fine." I stand tall. "I need to be back here by two for my next client." I clear my throat. "Or our next client?"

The ride in the limo to the hotel is quiet and aggravating; there is a conversation that needs to be said between us, but we aren't speaking at all. The Maître d' guides us to our table where Rachel is waiting with papers to sign. Rachel stands up with a weird look staring at us as we walk toward her; Brett looks at me with a fake smile.

"Good afternoon, Mr. Slade and Ms. Deel." "Lunch has been ordered already." Rachel beams. "Have a seat and let's get started, shall we?"

"Yes, Ms. Everly." Brett unbuttons his suit jacket and takes a seat at the table. "Let's get started." The Maître d' seats me next to Rachel across from Brett. *Oh joy, I get to look at the most confusing man I ever met.* "Are you ready Ms. Deel?"

"Yes." I say glumly. "I would like know what you'll do to us." Rachel gives me an unsettling look. "As a business partner." Brett knows exactly what I am referring to and the attraction I feel towards him is uncanny. He frowns a little.

"Okay, please read over your set of documents and mark anything you'll need to discuss or change with a yellow highlighter." Rachel continues in a professional manner with a curious smile. "And we will address each issue as they rise.

The waiter and waitress arrive with appetizers and drinks. Reading the contract, I look up at Brett waiting for him to give me a sign that he knows what we feel for each other isn't over, but he never did until the waiter came back to pick up plates from the appetizers. Brett gazes directly at me and smiles, my thrilled heart races; a tear of joy trickles down my cheek, I wipe it away and excuse myself from the table to get some air. Not long after Brett finds me outside, I turn to face him, and he wraps his arms around my waist.

"I am not going to lie to you." Brett steps inward and whispers to me. "This isn't my regular business practices." He sighs. "But..."

"What is it, Brett?" I ask frowning.

"If this...is going to work." He is doe-eyed. "I want try." I kiss him deeply and he returns the favor.

"Yes." I smile. "I do too." Rachel is smiling watching from the window.

"We'd better get back inside." Brett says. "The contracts are waiting." He takes my hand and we return to the table. I finish reading the contract.

"Okay, are you both finished reading the contract?" Rachel utters. "Are there any issues?"

"Yes." I slide the papers over to her. "Here Rachel, I've highlighted it."

"Oh, okay." She grimaces. "What's the problem?"

"It says if I go bankrupt." I add. "He can take my business away from me, right?"

"Yes." Rachel knew I wouldn't go for it. "That is correct."

"That needs to be changed." I state. "Or I won't sign it." His eyes shut.

"Mr. Slade, any issues with changing this portion of the contract?" Brett laughs a little.

"No, you can change it." He clears his throat. "But, in turn I'd like a say on the clientele list."

"What do you mean?" I give him glare at first. "Where it comes from?" Then sensually sigh. "Or what…extras are involved?"

"Both." Brett sneers intriguingly. "Is that alright Ms. Deel?"

"Only if we discuss the particulars privately." I smile. "Mr. Slade..."

"Yes, of course." He looks happy. "Ms. Deel."

"Great, let me note the changes." Rachel supplies trying to avoid their private conversation. "I'll bring you the corrected contracts later today."

"Thank you, Ms. Everly." Brett retorts seriously. "We will be at the salon, later."

We all finish lunch and part ways; Brett and I get in the limo to go back to the salon. I notice the driver is heading in a different direction and I wonder where we are going when I look at Brett.

"I want to show you something." He smiles taps the spot next to him, I slide over next to him. "Okay." "We have time for a little detour." I giggle. "Where are you taking me?"

"Home." He breaths and kisses me lightly on the lips. "My home."

"Okay." "…But we only have an hour." I kiss him back. "I have a client at two o'clock."

"I promise." He laughs. "You'll be back to the salon on time."

"I don't understand." My body shivers. "Why are we going to your home?"

"I told you." His face lightens. "I want to show you something." I nod. "Something special to me." I don't if I should be curious or scared.

When we arrive at his terra cotta colored mansion, it is breath takingly huge from the roadway to its half-circle driveway in front.

Brett opens the limo door and smiles, he takes my hand and we vacate the limo. The etched glass double doors to the foyer are amazing as we walk inside his home. Brett places his hand it on my lower back, it quickly sends tingles through my body; I shyly look up at his face, blush with feverish desire and his arm rolls me into his body closely, he smiles sweetly.

"Don't worry." His lips whisper and kisses me deeply. "We'll have plenty of time for us…later."

I make-believe smile, while inside a deep desperate passion wants to be unleashed, then he releases me from his side and leads us to a room next to the library. Brett slowly opens the door to his favorite room, we walk inside and my heart races with excitement. The room is filled with customized massage tables, oils and sexual toys on left side; the right side has a customized hot tub with specialized seating paraphernalia. I gasp looking around the room at all the items and he wraps his arms around my waist and I lean my back into his broad chest and smile.

"M-mm, I intend on testing…all these items…" Brett sizzles. "Before we use them on our special clientele." He breaths in my ear sending sparks to my brain.

"Oh-h, who will be…tested first?" My heart flutters. "Me or you?"

"Ladies first." He grimaces. "Or I can…if you want?"

"No…I'll go first." My heart begins to beat faster at the thought, I freeze and reality sets in. "But…we need to get back to the salon."

"Okay." Brett sighs. "I'll have all these items delivered to the salon." "By weeks' end."

"Sure." I feel my stomach swirling nervously. "But we really… need to go."

"Let's go." He turns placing his hand again on my lower back and leads me out of the room toward the front door. "The limo is waiting out front for you." "The driver will take you back to the salon."

"I thought you were going back with me." I pout. "To the salon."

"Not now." Brett clears his throat. "I have a few business calls to make and I'll join you later."

"Oh okay." I frown. "I see you at the salon later."

The drive back to the salon is quiet and nerve racking at the same time. As soon as I reach the front door to the salon, my two o'clock client is getting out of her car and standing behind me as I unlock it.

"Hello Darby." She says in broken English. "I thought you forgot my appointment." Dana is a tall, strong-minded middle-aged Filipino woman.

"Oh, no." I laugh. "Dana, I could never-ever forget you." We laugh together. "Come inside." "Sign-in and I'll get the room ready." We walk inside together and I quickly setup room one for her entrance. "Okay Dana, you know the routine." I set the stones in the warming bath. "I'll see you in a few minutes." Dana starts undressing before I shut the door behind me.

Meanwhile I go to my desk, the phone is blinking with messages; then as I reach it to hit the playback button the phone rings, startling me. The caller ID says Brett Slade, should I answer it or let it go to voice mail; without a second thought, he ditches me for business calls,

I'll ditch him for business. I walk away from my desk and enter room one with a quick knock.

"Are you ready Dana?" I blurt out, still hearing the phone ring again and again. "To start."

"Yes, Darby." She mumbles laying on her stomach. "My neck and back have been really stiff this week."

"Okay, I'll focus on those areas." I smile getting into my massage groove. "Have you been getting headaches too?"

"Yes." Dana sighs. "For last two days, almost migraines."

"I am going to start at your feet." I explain. "I'll hit a few pressure points on the way." "You let me know if it helps." I rub special oils on my hands and touch her toes. Brett slips inside the salon without me noticing.

"Okay, Darby." She quakes and fidgets a little.

"Now, relax and enjoy the massage." I say in soothing voice. I press on her arches of her feet.

"Mm-mm." Dana sighs. "Sounds heavenly."

Dana starts to drift off and I slowly rub the back of her legs, lower back and then I finish her back with strategically place the stones on her spine from buttocks to the nape of her neck.

"Don't move, Dana." I stretch my arms and hands. "I'll be back in five minutes."

"Huh-uh." I hear a soft mumble from the massage table, I giggle quietly and leave the room.

Upon shutting the room one door, Brett is standing inches away from me and I smile; he launches into my body, wrapping me into his and kisses my lips with heated passion leaving me breathless. Brett's fingers fumble with the first few buttons of my blouse, then he untucks it from my pants slides his hands underneath caressing my back pulling me closer against his frame. It feels like I am in the best sexual fantasy of my life, but realize where I am, my heart is racing faster and push him away quickly. My hand is pushes against his chest, holding him at bay; his eyes are full of desire and heat, then he breaths. I want to give in, then…I voice.

"Brett, we can't do this here." I say out of breath from this desirable embrace. "I have a client."

"Then…I am your next client." Brett breaths fiery. "I expect the…best you've got." He smirks touching my cheek with the back of his hand softly. "I'll be waiting in the office."

"Yes." I gasp with wanting. "I'll expect payment in full." Brett's hot frame still touching my body and I can feel his manhood throbbing against my thigh.

"No problem." He whispers in my ear. "If it's good…I'll come again and again."

"Oh-h." I kiss his sultry lips. "I think that's a workable deal." Brett walks away towards the office, I fix my blouse and return to room one.

"Okay, Dana." My chest hammers and my legs shake, as I try to regain my composure. "It's time to turn over." I remove the stones slowly and Dana turns over on the table.

"Darby, are you okay?" Dana stares. "You are flushed and sweaty."

"I am fine." I make a lame excuse, while spreading massage oil on the front of her legs. "I was testing the heating bed bulbs in room six and I was too close." Dana nods, but I know she doesn't believe me; she didn't say anything else until she hands me her credit card at the register.

"Darby." Dana says in a low voice. "If that handsome man in your office has anything to do with..." She points out with her index finger. "Girl...don't let me stop you." Dana smiles. "Bye." She leaves quickly out the front door and I go to room one to clean up.

A few moments later, Brett is standing directly behind me, touching my butt with his body and I can feel his hips moving his maleness with wanting against my bottom. His hands slide around to my breasts, caressing the nipples through my blouse; he breaths into my neck sending tingles down my spine and his lips touch my shoulder with searing desire. Brett's hands make their way to my pants, the undoing is complete; his caressing fingers reach my private place and I moan with pleasure.

"Darby." He sizzles. "I want you...now."

"Brett." I gasp sultry. "You said that you want my best." He eyes glimmer. "Get undress." I breath. "Be on the table in five." My voice gets shaky. "I'll be right back to give a massage you'll never forget." I walk out of the room slowly shutting the door behind me, never taking my eyes off him.

After locking the front door and shutting the lobby lights off; I enter the office and walk directly into the private bathroom to change clothes. Last year, Rachel held my birthday party here at the salon; she got me some slinky black lacey lingerie to wear for a someday special client, so I kept it in my locker at work. My heart beats faster as I reach inside to get it out, I anticipate that Brett may qualify as that special client if I can get past his self-righteous, cocky attitude. I feel amazingly in control when I slide the black lacy panties over my ladies' garden and the sexual thrill continues as I slip the lacy bra on to cover each breast. When I look in the mirror, I am not embarrassed at being almost naked, but feel fiery, strong and fearless. Without reservations, I leave the office and enter room one; Brett is laying down on the massage table on his back completely naked, smiling. I close the door behind me.

"I think you have the wrong idea." I say examining the view. "I am giving you a massage."

"Wow." He utters admiring his prospect, leaning up on his elbows. "A massage…with you dressed like..." Brett's eyes are glued. "Yea…ok a massage."

"Please turn over on your stomach." My voice shrills professionally. "And I can begin your incredible massage." He hesitates and turns over slowly.

"Darby." His face lays in the head piece. "This is not."

"Please be quiet." I cut him off daringly. "I will begin with warmed oils to help you relax."

"Okay." He mumbles face down.

I begin by pouring a small stream of oil on his muscular back, smearing it around with my hands, starting at his neck, shoulders and down the length of each arm. I rub in the oil deeply caressing his feet, up each leg, buttocks, not missing a spot. Brett's body is relaxing more every minute, until I reach his hips; my hands massage deeply into his groin area and he moans with pleasure.

"Time to rollover on your back." I breath. "Brett."

"Mm-mm." He complies slowly. "Darby."

I can feel my heart race as I watch him, my inner core pounds with wanting.

"Wow…" I whisper, my throat feels dry with fever.

Once again in control, I pour warm oil on his stomach and begin spreading it around his chest, shoulders and arms. Brett's eyes open slightly, he smiles, his hand slides up my right leg slowly, I place his arm back on the table and he shut his eyes again. Pouring more oil on my hands, I start the massage at the foot of the table beginning with his shins, pushing his legs open wider; my fingers go deeply massaging into the muscles all the way to his manhood, my face flushes more heatedly and my heart hammers in my chest. I never wanted to touch a man like this before, it is new territory for me and Brett seems like a man who gets what he wants when he wants it. I quickly back away from his growing investment and finish the massage.

"All done, Brett." I rush out, leaving the door open. "Time to get dressed."

"Darby." He stares at the open door. "Wait." Brett quickly slides off the table grabbing the discarded sheet off the floor and runs after me. "Darby." He stops me at the office doorway, I turn to him with tears in my eyes. "What's wrong?"

"I-I." Brett's passionate kiss cuts off my voice; his facial expression is sincere, but there is something cold behind it, that's what scares me, and I go stiff in his embrace; he realizes I am not ready and stops himself.

"I am going to get dressed." Brett smiles, but put-off. "You should too." He leaves the office to get his clothes in room one. I change clothes and return the garments to my locker, then I walk over to room one and Brett is staring at the table with a serious look.

"Brett, I am ready to go." I sigh. "home." He still stands there in silence, then his hand caresses the mat as he turns to face me.

"Darby." Brett smiles, and utters enlightened. "I want to cook dinner for you." His green eyes are beautiful, but serious. "Tonight?" He changes the subject and steps closer to me.

"Brett." I giggle with unsteady curiosity. "You cook?" I smile brightly. "Yes, I would love it." "I can make dessert?" His arms wrap around my waist, I hesitate a little after what happened.

"You are my dessert." Brett's kiss is soft and tingly; his touch is churns-up fierce sexual feelings.

"Uh-h, can you take me home…first?" I breath lightly.

"Yes." He breaths.

Brett takes my hand and we walk to the door; he gently takes the key from my fingers and locks the door behind us. We sit so close together in the vehicle, I can feel his heartbeat next to mine; time escapes us as the limo quickly takes us to my house. Brett, once again takes the keys from me and opens the door to my inner sanctum; I feel the sexual anticipation growing inside my passionate core as my desire for him builds. We walk inside hand and hand, he shuts the front door behind us; Brett swings me into his embrace, I look deeply into his eyes and smile, I want to be with him, but want to be in control. *What if I let go for one night and enjoy it?* I take a deep breath and smile. *It doesn't have to be forever, I can let him go.*

"Brett." I smirk with interest. "What will we do…to." His lips halt my words in a fiery kiss.

"Darling Darby." He smiles sensually. "I want to…" Brett breaths, stepping back a little from my body. "cook you, dinner." His lips utter. "Where's the kitchen?" I let go of his neck slowly, sliding my fingers down his muscular chest. *Why did he stop me?* My mind races as we pass my bedroom on the right side of the hallway. I feel him staring at my backside.

"Follow me." I mumble. "Brett." We walk down a short hallway to a room on the left. "Here is my kitchen." I point on the right. "Pots and pans are in the bottom of that cabinet." I sigh, and Brett wraps his arms around my waist from behind and stands very close to my frame. "The utensils are in the drawer…over there." Brett's left-hand cups my right breast and his fingers caress my nipple until it peaks. I breathlessly try to speak. "On the left…of the stove."

I feel his breath on my neck, he nibbles on my left ear; his right-hand slides down to my inner thigh and massages toward my avid lady's garden. I turn into his embrace, we kiss feverishly; stopping only a second, I look into his eyes I can see the warmth of his soul, beyond the frigidness and I let go of my fear. Brett quickly picks me up into his arms and carries me to my bedroom; it only takes seconds for us to disrobe and begin to make love for the first time. I touch him softly with my fingers caressing his maleness; he massages my inner thigh probing his finger gently into my fiery core; we moan together, passionately kissing, and playing into our heating advances. Brett reaches for a foil packet from his tossed away pants, he rips it with his teeth, sliding it quickly over his maleness and he climbs on top of me plunging his hardened manhood forward into my cavern of liquid desire. We move like waves in the ocean, back and forth, over and over; his hands draw my buttock s into to him, then our swells develop into one strong forwarding thrust of liquid intensity sending us into a euphoric bliss.

"Oh…Brett." I say passionately aloud.

"Oh, Darby." Brett purges on his release. "You're so beautiful." His kisses leave me breathless and rolls off to my side. I snuggle in close to his chest and we fall asleep until the morning sun peaks through my window curtains.

"Hey…Brett." I whisper looking at his resting form. "I want food." His eyes peek open, he laughs and smiles.

"Good morning, beautiful." Brett kisses me. "Yeah…I am hungry too." He stretches his lengthy frame. "Do you want to help me…" His eyebrows raise. "Cook?"

I shift my body slightly to face him. "Yes, I'd love to help you." I yawn and smile.

Brett gets out of my bed, he puts on his underwear and slides on his black slacks. I put on my panties and reach for his blue dress shirt, put it on to cover my bare breasts; he stares at me as I button it up to my cleavage and smiles. We walk out of my room together, his hand slides to my lower back and I feel sexually alive from his touch.

"My shirt never looked so amazing." He mumbles. "I think I could get used to seeing you like this."

"Thank you." I breath in the smell of his enticing cologne on his dress shirt. "Let's make breakfast."

As we enter the kitchen, Brett goes directly to the refrigerator to inspect its ingredients; I go to the cabinets near the sink where the coffee pot is located, pulling the coffee and filter out to prepare its dark sustenance. He finds eggs, shredded cheese, onions, ham and peppers.; puts them on the counter top and smiles.

"Darby." "Do you like omelets?" His voice crackles. "I make a mean western omelet."

"Yes, I do." I smile. "Do you want coffee?" I blurb out. "Or tea?"

"Coffee is fine." He's looking around the kitchen. "Where is the cutting board?"

"Here." I hand him the cutting board from the dishwasher. "And the knives are in the drawer next to the stove."

"Thank you." Brett's sensual stare makes me tingle. "By the way." "I take my coffee black with two sugars." I stroll over to Brett side.

"Okay." "The coffee is brewing." "Is there something…" I stand very close to his side. "I can help you with?" Brett looks right at me and smiles. "Do you want me…" My voice is blocked by his lips; his kiss sends me into a heated spiral.

"Oh, I want you…Darby." Brett utters in between kisses, then he stops. "But I want to eat first." I sigh.

"Can you scramble the eggs?" He asks. "I'll chop up the veggies." I nod without moving my body.

"I will, but…" I whisper in his ear. "I owe you dessert."

"Don't worry." He spicily stares. "I will collect."

"Okay." I grab a mixing bowl out the cabinet next to the stove and begin cracking eggs into it. "I'll have these ready in a few minutes." Brett starts humming a song while he chops up onions and peppers. "That sounds nice." I ask staring at him. "What song is that?"

"I can love you like that" by All 4 One." "It's a song from the nineties." He continues to hum it. I hand him the bowl with the eggs scrambled. "Thank you." His lips touch mine once again, this time I pull him in closer and kiss him back. "Darby." "You are so beautiful." He breaths. "I don't know if…" I look at him confused. "Never mind." "Let's eat."

He stirs the ingredients together in the scrambled eggs; I pull the frying pan out from the bottom cabinet next to the stove and hand it to him. I give him a sad confused look; he gives me a sympathetic smile and continues preparing the omelets. I am lost in thought as I sit down on a chair at the kitchen table and Brett is at the stove cooking the omelets, humming the same song again. *It feels like torcher not knowing if he wants us to be, or not and what is he really hiding from me; I haven't felt this way for someone in a long time and it scares me.* I hear him speaking to me, but my thoughts are so deep that it sounds like murmuring not words; Brett clears his throat to get my attention and walks toward me with a plate of food.

"Darby." "Are you okay?" He looks torn, but smiles. "Here's your omelet." He sits across from me at the table. "I know you feel something for me." "But I."

"But, what?" "Brett." I touch his hands across the table.

"We can't be…a couple." He gets administrative. "We are working in business together."

"I know that…" I state clearly. "But we…can try"

I pick up my fork and start to eat the delicious omelet, I let my mind drift off the subject. Brett stares at first and begins to eat his omelet too. We do not speak about this again, working together we clean the dishes and put them away; then we prepare to go to the Big

Bay Hotel to get things rolling on the reopening of the Resort and Spa. Brett notices that I am distant but tries to ignore it; we arrive at the Hotel in his limo, concierge meets us at the door.

"Mr. Slade and Ms. Deel." "Mr. Bosworth is waiting in his office." The well-dressed lady directs us to the elevator. "Please follow me."

We get into the elevator and ride it to the fifteenth floor; the doors open to beautifully decorated office; the secretary welcomes us and concierge leaves in the elevator to return to her desk.

"Mr. Bosworth is in the conference room." The secretary smiles. "Please follow me."

We walk down the hallway to a set of double doors decorated with two huge calligraphic B's that almost covered each door. The secretary opens the doors and waves us inside.

"Please come in and take a seat anywhere." The tall fairly, good-looking dark-haired man utters standing beside a long conference table. "So, we can start our meeting." "Ms. Deel." "Mr. Slade."

"Thank you, Mr. Bosworth." Brett speaks strongly. "Miss. Deel and I." He eyes brightly smile. "We are excited to be here."

"Okay, let's get started." Bosworth announces buzzing his secretary on the speaker phone. "Marcy, please bring in the contracts."

"Yes, Sir." The receiver clicks off.

"Firstly, Otis." "Please call me Darby." I say kindly. "Since, we already know each other." Bosworth nods.

"I agree with Darby." Brett grimaces. "Mr. Bosworth." "First name basis makes this friendlier." "Call me Brett."

"Yes, good idea." His hand reaches out to Brett. "Otis."

Marcy walks in the conference room holding three sets of paperwork, passing out a set to each one of us; then leaves closing the door behind her. Otis smiles and opens his packet to review. Brett and I follow his lead and open our packets too. The conversion discussion starts, we continue throughout the afternoon and into early evening; finally, we come to an agreement. Marcy rewrites the contracts with all the agreed changes and we sign them.

"Okay, now that the deal is done." Otis spouts with a smile. "Darby and Brett, will you join me for dinner downstairs?"

"Yes, I would love too." I smile. "Thank you." "Brett?" Otis asks politely.

"No, I need to go to my office." He says smartly. "But, thanks for asking."

We quietly ride the elevator down to the first floor. Otis and I walk out of the elevator toward the dining room; Brett grabs my arm softly, to stop me and stares.

"What is it?" I see he looks upset, sad even. "Brett."

"Darby, call me when your done with dinner." He speaks softly. "I need to talk to you."

"Why?" I stare a little confused. "Say whatever it is." "I-I." Brett shuts his eyes. "Please call me." He walks away and I'm still, watching him walk away.

"Darby, are you coming?" Otis states aloud.

"Yes, sorry." I take a deep breath. "I am."

The dinner goes well, Otis and I talk about the renovation and advertising ideas. When dessert comes, I drift away in thought and remember the first time I danced with Brett in this very ballroom, how his touch sent tingles everywhere inside me. Otis notices that I've veered away from the conversation and smiles.

"Is it a good memory?" Otis asks. "Darby."

"What?" "Huh." I feel embarrassed. "I am sorry, Otis."

"Are you okay?" Otis frowns.

"Yes, but I need to go." I spout. "Thanks for dinner."

I leave the dining area, walk into the lobby, pulling my phone out of my jacket and then I look up; Brett is standing there only two feet from me, smiling with his hand out for me to take. We walk outside to his waiting limo before we enter the vehicle he pulls me close and kisses me. I get inside the limo first and he follows; he sits next to me and stares out in space.

"We need to talk, Darby." His voice gruffly shakes. "I am in uncharted territory." I touch his hand and smile.

"It is okay to care for me." I say softly. "I have feelings for you too." Our eyes meet and his lips shimmy.

"But…I never mix business with pleasure." Brett says roughly. "And I don't know…" He sighs.

“I am not just pleasure.” I take a deep breath, holding back the fear. “Am I?”

“I-I can’t…” He leans back against the seat. “Darby.” “After I left you here.” His voice stops.

“Yes, Brett.” My heart is racing. “Tell me.”

“I couldn’t stand it.” Brett takes my hands. “You, having dinner with another man.” I giggle.

“Don’t be silly.” I kiss his cheek. “Otis and I have been friends for years.” Brett looks serious. “I have no interest in Otis.” “No need to be jealous.”

“I am not jealous, Darby.” Brett snarls. “I am selfish.” “I want you to myself.” His kiss is forceful and strong, leaving me breathless.

“Brett.” I push him away. “Easy tiger, not so rough.”

“Darby, please come home with me?” He is eager.

“Spend the night.” I feel uncomfortable after the intense kiss.

“I can’t tonight.” I move away. “Early client tomorrow.” “Your brother Will.” He stares.

“Will?” “He has an appointment with you.” Brett frowns with displeasure. “I told him to check-out the business, not partake.”

“Well, I guess I give an impressive massage.” Smiling and he glares, I sit back against the seat and the limo stops a few moments later. “Where are we?”

“My house.” Brett sighs. “Come in for a little while.” “And I’ll have the driver take you home later.”

“No.” I stay back against the seat. “I’d like to go home, please.”

“Please.” Brett shifts in his seat. “Come in.” “I promise to behave.” He opens the door and reaches for my hand. I apprehensively take his hand and get out of the vehicle. “Thank you, Darby.”

“I’m trusting you.” I take his arm and we walk into his house. “And please don’t lie to me.”

"I won't." "Would you like a nightcap?" As we walk into his study, I sit on the rather large sofa and Brett pours liquor into two glasses. "Here you go." I take the drink and he sits next to me.

"What did you mean by selfish?" I inquire.

"Honestly, I don't know." Brett squirms a little. "I want this." He kisses me softly. "And this." I laugh wrapping my arms around his neck and kiss him again. "But I am not sure if I can…"

"Be in a relationship." I smile, assumingly. "This is the beginning of something real." "We both feel it."

"I am afraid." He clears his throat. "You won't like my peculiar ways."

"What do you mean?" I am curious. "Sexually or?"

"Both." He looks serious. "I enjoy being a freeman, but I want to be with you too." Surprisingly, I stare with interest.

"Go on." I utter.

"I don't want to share you with anyone." His voice wavers. "You are only…a part of my pleasure." A new fear washes over me, should I partake or not. He voices. "I like orges with multiple partners, enjoy getting-off."

"Brett, I want to go home." I spat out quickly, and he falls back against the sofa. "Please." Brett sighs, stands up and reaches for my hand; he leads me to the front door.

"Darby." Brett kisses me softly. "Don't be afraid." "I would never hurt you." I nod.

"I need to think about it." I try to smile. "See you at the salon tomorrow." He nods as I walk out to the limo, get inside and drive away. "Driver, take me to the salon." I speak to the lowered window between us. "I need to pick up my car."

"Yes Ma'am." The deep voice rumbles. "We will be there shortly." I smile.

Once I enter my home, I sense loss and sadness; his words are repeating in my mind, I do not know if I can do what he wants. In my mind, I picture whips, handcuffs and chains; only pleasure, torture and pain. I shower before bed, in my exhausting state I fall asleep quickly until the morning light peeks through my bedroom curtains, waking me again. Brett and I have only been together for a short time, but I feel I am losing control of who I am. I realize that I am not experienced in what sexual pleasures he wants/needs, but maybe I should try. I dress in my salon attire and go to the kitchen for breakfast; then I leave for work. *Maybe, I should talk to Will, he is Brett's brother. I thought.* I reach the salon, there are four moving trucks waiting out front and Will is standing by his car.

"What is going?" I stand outside my car door and close it. "Can I help you?"

"Are you Ms. Deel?" The guy from the first truck asks.

"Yes." I say.

"Mr. Slade asked us to deliver these items to the salon." The guy continues. "Where would you like the?"

"Wow, four trucks." I am stunned. "That's a lot of stuff." "Give me a few minutes to clear out a room."

"Let us help." The guy gets out of his truck. "Mr. Slade insists."

"Okay, follow me." The four drivers and their assistants follow me inside the salon after I unlock the door. "Will, you can sign in and go to room one." "I'll be there shortly."

"Are sure Darby?" Will smiles. "I can reschedule." "You look pretty busy."

"No, this shouldn't take too long." I state. "If you don't mind waiting."

"I don't." Will walks toward room one. "See you soon."

Will is smiling while watching me direct traffic into room seven, then he goes inside room one to ready himself for a massage. I direct the first two of the men to move the massage table into room four, the next two to move the water bath into the basement after they empty the water bath outside, the following two men to move the sheet and towel chaffier robe to the supply room and the last two men could go unpack the first truck. Brett quietly slips inside the salon without me noticing, he sees Will walking into room one and goes inside the room a few minutes later.

"If you have any questions." I say aloud. "Please do not hesitate to knock on room one."

"Yes, Ma'am." The guy from the first truck replies.

"Will, are you ready?" I knock on the door to room one. "Will?" No answer from inside, so I open the door slowly. Will is sitting on the massage table with his clothes on and Brett is standing against the wall in the corner. "What's going on in here?" They stare at each other and then look at me. "Well, someone answer me."

"Darby, I am sorry." Will speaks first. "I need to reschedule this appointment." He gets off the table and leaves the room.

"Will, wait." I try to stop him. "I don't understand."

"What is it…about you that?" Brett spills out.

"That…what?" I glare at Brett.

"Makes you care." He blurts out. "So much."

"Wait, Will." I walk quickly out the door and Brett follows.

"Darby, stop!" Brett strongly grabs my arm.

"Brett, let-me-go." I give him angry look. "I have a job to do." He releases me, and I walk to my desk. "Will, what day would you like and time?" Will looks behind me at Brett and back to me.

"Darby." Will smiles. "I'll call you later." He leaves the salon.

"Brett, what is wrong with you?" My eyes are ready to burn his face. "You're acting crazy."

"My brother likes you." Brett tries to explain without getting angry. "Too-much."

"Yes, he's very nice." I retort calm.

"I don't trust him." He looks enraged, but he keeps his cool. "With you."

"Why?" "I'm confused." I'm beginning to unravel as the anger flows. "First, you want me." "Then you don't, then you do again." Now, the anger is steam rolling out of my mouth. "And now…you don't think that I'll like your sexual flavors." I continue shrilling. "Today, you!" "Made us lose business over jealousy." "Why?"

"He's my brother." Brett supplies upset. "I don't trust him with you."

"Not good enough!" "Why?" I ask determined to get answer.

Brett shakes his head no. I walk away, heading into my office, slide around my desk; the tears of confusion wash over me, collapsing into my office chair and I shut my eyes. I can feel him in the room, he shuts the door behind him and takes a seat in one of the chairs in front of my desk. I sit still with strange sexual absurdities running through my head, when Brett decides to speak; his voice shakes, but it starts to calm down.

"I know it is confusing." His hands shake trying to reach out to me. "And I am sorry that I-I."

"That you dropped a bomb on me." I talk trying not to sob. "Right now." I sigh. "There is no explanation that I want to here, so please leave me alone."

"But, I want to tell you…"

"Brett, please leave." I stand up from my chair. "Go help your movers." I walk around my desk towards the door. "I have a client in fifteen minutes." Open the door and leave him standing there alone; Nancy is signing in at the desk smiling, she hands me a release paper signed by her doctor allowing her to be here.

"Darby, how are you?" Nancy says blissfully, until she sees my sad face. "Oh girl, what's wrong?"

"It is nothing, things change." I try to smile. "How are you feeling?"

"Doctor said, I need to relax more and less stress." Nancy supplies saddened. "I retired yesterday." "Thirty years on the job."

"Wow, that's a long time." "Are you ready for your massage?" I sputter. "Any specific areas you want me to work on?"

"Yes, the same areas as last week." Nancy smirks. "And my neck feels a little tight, too."

"Okay, let me check you in." I smile back to her. "Go into room two, get ready and I'll be in there soon."

"Okay Darby." Nancy strolls away.

Brett waits for Nancy to close the door to room two and walks out of the office; he stands behind me, wraps his arms around my waist and kisses my neck. I want to pull his arms away, but I don't. His body feels so good against mine and his lips touching my neck sends tingles to my intimate core.

> "Don't move." Brett whispers. "I want to say something." My body stiffens, I shut my eyes and listen. "This is what I need from you." I nod. "Trust." "I know my sexual lifestyle scares you." He continues. "But it is about pleasure, not love." "Do you understand?" I nod again. "I care a lot about you." "That's why I am selfish." "And want to share this…with you." Brett releases me and walks away to room seven. I let out a heavy sigh, wiping the tears from my eyes and walk to room two.
>
> "Nancy, are you ready?" I say knocking. "Nancy." I open the door, she's down on the floor not moving and I rush over to her side, checking for a pulse and I can't feel it. "Brett!" I scream. "Call 9-1-1!" "Brett!" My heart is racing. Brett runs from room seven with his cellphone stuck to his ear to room two.
>
> "We need an ambulance to Bare Day Salon, now!" Brett announces clearly. "Nancy is unconscious, not breathing and…" I am holding my two fingers on her left wrist; the tears are running down my cheeks and I feel like can't breathe. "No pulse."
>
> "We are on the way." The dispatcher says. "Don't hang up."

Brett drops the phone in his hand to the floor, he's at my side in seconds, holding me against his frame and comforting me from the sadness I feel. The ambulance arrives with the police in tow, the police contact George, directing him to the hospital and Nancy is gone, she died of a massive heart attack. The policeman takes my statement a few moments later and they leave the salon. Brett helps me to my feet, we walk slowly to the office and I lay on the sofa with my head in his lap as he hands me Kleenex to wipe my unending tears.

"Darby, it's going to be okay." Brett speaks softly. "Nancy lived a good life."

"Poor George, he'll be crushed." I sniff. "And she was my first client." I sit up next to him.

"Don't worry." He's trying to be positive. "Beside once we get this salon up to date." "We'll be so busy." "You won't have to worry anymore." I kiss him softly on the lips.

"Sometimes you can be the sweetest man ever." He returns the kiss with passion. "And the most confusing too."

"You are my alleles heel." Brett breaths. "So beautiful and smart." The kisses start to generate sexual heat between us, but I stop it. We stand up together, I leave the office swiftly and he stares. "Darby." "Wait."

I return to room two to clean up after the paramedics left, seeing Nancy's purse on the chair and knowing that I would have to contact George at some point to retrieve it; I start to cry again, feeling overwhelmed by Nancy's death, Brett's secret lifestyle and the decisions that await my approval; emotionally I collapse to the floor curling to the fetal position in tears until I am washed out. I slowly return to my feet, walk to my office to use the private restroom and I stare into the mirror before I wash my tear ridden face. The cool water feels great on my face when someone walks in my office; I grab the hand towel and dry my face.

"Excuse me, Ms. Deel." The lead mover says unsure a few minutes later. "Sorry to bother you." "Mr. Slade wants you to decide where the hot tub goes." I pull the towel away; the man smiles sympathetically.

"Oh okay, give me a few minutes." I state trying to regain my composure. "I'll let you know what room to put it in."

"Sure." "We will be working in room seven." He smirks. "Thank you." He walks away from the doorway. A great distraction from me feeling sad for George and sorry for myself, work.

"Umm, what room has the plumbing for the tub?" I walk out of the office and I remember room ten has two big sinks in it. "Excuse me, Sir." I look through the doorway of room seven. "Come with me, if you would." He follows me to room ten. "Do you think this room will work." The lead man smiles at the sinks. "For the hot tub?"

"Yes, this room will work." He laughs. "No need for a plumber." "Okay." The man lets out a heavy sigh. "We are finishing up in seven." "And I'll have the guys unpack the tub." Brett is standing in the office doorway with a serious look on his face.

"That's great, let me know if you need anything else." I walk towards Brett with a fake smile.

"Sure will." The man returns to room seven.

"What's wrong, Brett?" I ask sassy. "I am not falling all over you."

"I am not angry about that." "Darby." Brett sighs roughly taking my hand, leading me into the office and shutting the door behind us. "I have to leave the country for a few months."

"Why?" I stare at him. "We haven't started the new clientele list or updated the salon yet."

"I know." "But the pieces are here." He spouts smartly. "I have an old friend, she has agreed to come here, to help you set up and get the client list started."

"Okay, but one person isn't enough for the set up." I explain. "How?"

"Don't worry." Brett looks a little stiff. "Abby, has her own crew to help." He shifts his weight. "Matter of fact, she'll be here in a few hours."

"Are you going to be here?" I say nervous. "I don't…to introduce me."

"Yes." Brett smiles. "My flight leaves in the morning." I feel relief. "The movers are almost finished." "Would you like to have lunch with me?"

"Yes, I am hungry." I declare unsure of the intention from him. "Let's go check on the movers." Brett places his hand on my lower back, it sends sparking surges through my body and my legs quiver; we walk together to room ten.

"Are you okay?" He notices before we reach the door way. "You look…"

"Yes." I stop him, trying to avoid the subject of sex. "It's…" "Never mind." The problem is Brett, he excites me too easily; but, I didn't give in this time.

"Hey gentlemen, are you almost done setting up the hot tub?" Brett asks the lead mover.

"Yes, Sir." The lead man gestures. "We are getting ready to run a water test on the tub jets and drainage." He adds. "It shouldn't take more than an hour."

"Great." Brett stops mid-sentence his cellphone is vibrating. "If you have any questions." "Please ask Darby or myself." "Excuse me, I need to answer this call." He smiles, walking outside the salon. "Hello Abby."

"Okay, I'll be in my office." I leave the doorway, walking slowly towards the office curious to know who has Brett's attention outside the salon. "If you need anything."

I sit in my office chair behind my desk, thinking about Brett and everything that's transpired; until the phone rings shaking from my trance, I pick up the receiver and speak.

"Hello, Bare Day Salon." I sound chipper. "This is Darby." "How can I help you?"

"Darby, it's Brett." "Sorry, I am calling from the limo." He utters. "Abby's flight is arriving early, and I am on the way to pick her up."

"Okay, what about lunch?" I ask.

"No worries." Brett tells. "I'll pick you up on the way back from the airport."

"Sure." "I'll be here." I say sadly, after the call disconnects. "Waiting." After hanging up the receiver, I sit for a while longer thinking about Brett.

"Ms. Deel, would you please come to room ten?" One assistant mover asks. "We want you to check out the hot tub."

"Oh, okay." I stand up and walk out the office door. "I am on the way."

They finish hooking up the hot tub, the jets are running perfect, the temperature is set at one hundred four degrees and it is draining correctly. The movers pick up the trash, tools; they also move the items removed from room ten into the basement for storage. I sign-off on the invoice, they leave the salon and I am alone again. I decide to snoop in the boxes left in room seven, view the special massage tables and chairs. In one box there is slinky lingerie, including bras and panties; the next box has little sexual trinkets, such as prostate massagers, clit clips, dildos, nipple stimulators, penis rings and honey powder. I am so interested in snooping at the items in the boxes, that I didn't hear the phone ring or someone entering the salon until a female voice startles me out of my secret investigation. I turn around to see a young woman dressed in blue jeans and ripped red t-shirt standing behind me. Brett walks up behind her, looking directly at me. No introduction is needed, Abby is a beautiful blonde bombshell with long legs and a voice that could drip with honey or stab you viscously with a knife.

"Wow." Abby states tartly. "A virgin." She gnarls at me and looks back to Brett. "Are you going soft my boy?" "Huh."

"Abby, be nice." Brett smiles at me. "That's why you're here… to help her set up the salon." He clears his throat. "And maybe teach her a few tricks of the trade."

"Oh-h, this is going to be…fun." Abby slithers over to me and sliding her index finger of her right hand down my cheek sensually. "Baby Girl." "You are in for a treat." I step back from her and give Brett the evil eye.

"Now Abby, play nice." Brett squeals. "Darby, can I talk to you in the office?" I nod with a strangling intention. "Abby, get acquainted with the salon." He places his hand on my lower back. "Darby and I will be back shortly." *Not if I kill you first. I thought.* But then again, his touch sends my body spiraling sexually. "Darby." "I am sorry." Brett says as we enter the office. "Abby can be a little overboard."

"A little overboard…is that what you call it." I say huffy. "I'd call it being a total bitch."

"Darby." "She is rough talking on the outside." He says in her defense. "I know her." "She acts all bad."

"Yes." "And you defend her." I throw my hands up. "What happens to me when you leave?" "I-I."

"Nothing." "You'll be working together." Brett adds. "Abby… will help you." He kisses me.

"Brett, stop." I push him away. "I can't."

"You can't, what?" Brett kisses me again deeper and stronger this time; I return the favor passionately. "Oh-h." He breaths.

"Brett." I utter breathless. "We can't…Abby." He backs off. "Is here."

"You're right." Brett sighs. "You should go set up with Abby." "I have things to do before I leave in the morning." I start to walk away, and he reaches for my hand. "But, I want to be with you tonight." He pulls me close to him again. "Darby." I kiss him softly and smile.

"Okay Brett." My heart hammers in my chest. "Tonight." "But, we need to get Abby settled first."

"Let's go." Brett walks out the office door first and I follow. "Abby, should be in room seven." We walk together. "Hey Abby." Brett announces entering room seven. "Is everything here?"

"Yeah." Abby laughs. "It looks like it." She smiles at me. "Hey Darby, I'm sorry." "I came off like a bitch in heat." Her eyes turn to Brett then back at me. "He's been my friend for years." "I am a little over protective."

"I understand." I stand strong. "But this has to stop." I state. "If we are going to work together." Abby nods and Brett smiles.

"Ladies." "Let's get to work." Brett commands standing tall. "And I'll return in a few hours." He lifts his left brow. "Abby, I already reserved a room for you at the Big Bay Hotel."

"Great." Abby smiles seductively at him. "Did you run out of space in your mansion?"

"No, I did not." Brett stands closer to me. "We are working together, and it wouldn't be appropriate."

"Well, that didn't stop you before." Abby snarls sinfully.

"I am not living in the past, Abby." He debates. "Neither should you." My heart leaps, I realize that he is totally into me.

"Life lessons, again." Abby sighs ruffled. "You're a bummer, Brett." She reaches for my hand. "Let's get to work, Darby." We walk to the boxes lining the back wall and Brett leaves us. "Good, he's gone." Abby utters. "Darby, you've got a hold on him."

"What do you mean, Abby?" I stare at her.

"I've known him for a long time." Abby tares into the box in front of her. "Darby, he doesn't ever fall in love." "But I've never seen him like this with any woman, ever.'

"What?" My heart races. "Do you really think so?"

"Yeah." Abby growls with a smile. "And it pisses me off." We laugh together. "Okay, let's finish unpacking these boxes."

The items we unpacked from the boxes filled the floor. We separate quantities of each items per dresser for the four designated special client rooms. Abby and I move the four dressers to each room; then fill the six drawers with separated items, including various oils for massaging. Also, Brett had ordered eight black wood mesh woven design freestanding three-panel folding privacy screen room dividers, that will be used to conceal the Masseuse changing into slinky lingerie. Abby and I carry four of the room dividers into the rooms designated for our special clients, I attach the metal rods to each divider and hang the slinky items on them. Once we've finish moving the dressers closer to the black woven panels, we move the other four to room ten to be positioned around the hot tub for privacy. Abby walks outside room ten, she calls someone on her cellphone and smiles.

"Darby." Abby returns, still smiling. "My friends will be arriving in a few minutes to rearrange the new massage tables in the rooms." She continues. "And any other heavy lifting we need."

"Okay, sound great." I agree. "Hey Abby, are you hungry?" I ask. "I could order pizza."

"I am starving." She looks at me. "Pizza is perfect." "But you'll have order at least six pies."

"Why, six?" I frown.

"My friends are body builders." She laughs. "They eat a lot."

"Sure, six pizzas." I walk out of the room. "I'll call from my office."

I grab the phone off its receiver and dial my favorite pizza joint to place the order. The owner answers, he places my order and hangs up; I sit in my chair behind the desk and my thoughts run to Brett; he is falling for me, I can feel my heart race and my core tingles with desire. I shut my eyes for a moment, the smell of Brett's cologne flows through the room and his fingers touch my neck as he pushes my hair to the side.

"Darby." Brett breaths on my neck, sending tingles down my spine. "You are so beautiful." I place my hand on the side of his face, pulling it closer to my neck.

"Brett." I sigh sensually. "Your back early." He turns my chair to face him and lifts me up into his arms.

"I finished early and I…" Brett stops when Abby enters the office.

"The pizza delivery…guy." Abby stares. "Oops, sorry." She adds. "You need to pay for the pizzas, Darby."

"Thanks, Abby." I clear my throat and grab my wallet from my bag in the bottom drawer. "I'll be right back, Brett." I walk out of the office.

"What in the hell are you doing, Brett?" Abby says sternly in a low growl. "She's your partner in business."

"I know." Brett glares at Abby. "I shouldn't, but…"

"This is not like you." Abby continues angrily. "Unless, you're in love with her."

"I feel something for her and..." Brett halts when I return to the office, he smiles and walks over to me. "Darby."

"Pizza is here." I announce. "I am starving, let's eat."

Brett takes my hand, we walk out to the lobby and Abby follows. Abby's friends arrive shortly after, they join us for pizza; then they start rearranging the new massage tables in the rooms, then stacking the old ones in the basement to make more room. Abby walks her friends outside the salon, while Brett and I clean up the trash from dinner. The three of us get into Brett's limo, we drop Abby off at the hotel and drive to my house. Before, we reach my house, Brett wraps his arms around me; he kisses me passionately, then fumbles with the buttons on my blouse and I struggle with his. We cease long enough to feel the limo stop, climb out of the vehicle and unlock my front door. I shut the door behind us, grab him by the dress shirt and yank him close. I try to unbutton his shirt, but I can't and tear it off him instead. Brett is successful undoing my buttons, releasing my breasts from my bra while I release his pants to the floor and massage his garmented manhood. He slides his hands to my hips, releasing the button and zipper of my skirt letting it drop to floor next to his pants. Brett swats down to the floor, sliding my undergarments down with his hands and he takes them off at my feet; then he strokes my legs slowly upward, searing my skin with his heated kisses and continues until he reaches my fiery intimate place. I moan with desire, grabbing his head, pulling it in closer to my passion place; he moves up to my stomach placing more heated pecks until he reaches a breast to suckle and nibble, making me gasp for more. I grasp his face in my hands, pulling him up for a flaming kiss that left us breathless; my hand slid down to his briefs that caged his hot throbbing rod, pulling the briefs off his hip and using my foot to drop them on the clothing heap below. Brett lifts me up, wrapping my legs around his hips and carries me to my bed; he is ready to take charge until I roll on top and take control. I take a condom out of my night stand draw, tear the packaging with my teeth and sliding it over his hardened shaft.

"It's my turn." I utter breathless and he smiles.

Our drive starts slowly, enjoying each touch, riding up and down from a trot progressing to a canter into a full gallop and ending euphorically in an orgasm. I collapse on his heated chest, breathless and sweaty; then I roll to his side and fall asleep. Sometime in the early morning, Brett and I make love again, this time it is more amazing than before; we are left breathless, shaking from our orgasmic eruption wrap in each other's arms exhausted. I start to fall asleep again, until I hear him whispering and I smile.

> "You probably won't remember this." His voice whispers in the air. "I think I'm falling in love with you." His arms warmly tighten around me, and he falls asleep.

I wake after sunrise, the bed next to me is bare and Brett's gone; I walk slowly out of the bedroom with my bathrobe on, the clothes are gone from the floor by the front door; my skirt, blouse and undergarments are neatly lying over the top of a living room chair. I catch a whiff of fresh brewed coffee from the kitchen, my heart races and I quickly walk to the kitchen hoping he is still here. Upon entering the kitchen, it is empty except for a hot pot of coffee and a note on the counter. It read: "Darby, sorry I left without saying goodbye. I will return in a few months. Abby will help you get started with the client list, teach you how to manage the clientele and use the materials given. Don't worry. I won't forget you owe me dessert. I plan to collect in full upon my return. Love, Brett." The tears form on the edges of my eyes and hold the note close to my chest. I whisper. *"He loves me."* I pour myself a cup of coffee in a happy daze; then anxiety shakes me realizing that I will be working with Abby until Brett returns, how will I ever survive. Slowly, I stroll back to my bedroom to get ready for work, the phone rings and I pick it up from my dresser.

"Hello." I say while shoving my legs into a pair of blue jeans. "Who is it?" The phone starts to slide off my shoulder.

"Darby, it's Rachel." Her voice crackles. "Are you there?"

"Yeah." The phone drops and I catch it before it hits the floor. "Hold on Rach…I'm losing the phone." I put the phone against my ear. "Sorry girl." "What's up?"

"Mr. Sloan called me this morning." Rachel says. "He wants Abigale Steed on your payroll." I hear apprehension in her voice.

"Who is she?"

"Abby is a friend of Brett's." I mumble. "She's here to help me set up the salon."

"Oh, okay." She laughs. "You sound upset." "Is she a bitch?"

"Let's say, she didn't make a great first impression." I utter. "But really, Abby's not totally terrible."

"Sure Darby." Rachel adds not convinced. "Do you want to meet for lunch today?"

"Yes." "If you're not busy." I ask, tucking my shirt into my jeans. "Why don't come to the salon and help us set it up?"

"I have only one meeting this morning and nothing else scheduled." She pauses. "Sounds like fun." "Plus, I'd like to meet Abby."

"Great." I feel relief. "See you after your meeting, bye." I place the receiver back on its cradle and finish putting on my shoes.

The drive to the spa was quick, until I reach the parking lot of the Big Bay Hotel. There are cop cars everywhere, the lights flashing a blue blur and the police officers running inside the hotel with weapons ready. I drive past the blocked parking lot and park next to the salon in my usual spot, watching the commotion from a safe distance and I get out of my car. My first thoughts ran to Abby, hoping that she is all right and then Otis.

"Excuse me." A voice startles me. "Ms. Deel." I turn to my left to see a young handsome Policeman. "I am sorry, you'll have to move your car farther away from the hotel."

"Why?" "What's going on?" I see a concerning look.

"It's for your safety Miss." He exclaims. "Please move the vehicle."

"Yes Sir." I reply. "But you need to tell me what's going on?" I get back inside my car and start it.

"There may be a bomb on the premises." The policeman ushers me away. "Park on the backside of the spa." I wave in reply, driving around the building to park and go inside the backdoor.

Inside the salon, I can hear people talking in my office; I cannot recognize the voices, except for Abby's. *Who are these people and what are they doing in my salon?* I listen in, hoping to understand the conversation. The man is rambling on about the spa's location, the lady is mad because the client list is small to say the least and Abby is trying to calm them down. I am guessing investors or something else.

"Listen, you two." Abby spats. "Darby should be here soon." "I think she'll be able to clarify the vision."

"What do we know about this woman?" The man utters. "Or is he leading us by his dick again?"

"Detrick, that's not cool." The lady counters with European accent. "You know he has a big dick, darling." I peer around the doorway.

"Okay enough." Abby says upset. "Battering."

"Yes, please." I announce my arrival. "Brett is not a topic of this conversation." "Good morning Abby." I smile. "Who do we have here?" She smiles back.

"Darby." She directs my attention to my left. "This is Detrick." I see a mysteriously dark handsome man hidden under a hard-ridden exterior. Then she points to my right. "This is Mamie." I see a sophisticatedly dressed Asian lady with a sexual temptress lurking inside. "They are friends and fellow masseuses of Brett and I." "Paige, Jimmy and Alex will be here soon." "Their flight was delayed last night." I smile.

"Oh." I spout giddy. "By the way Brett would be delighted you speak so highly of…his penis." We all laugh.

"Okay, the formalities are out of the way." Abby smiles at me. "Darby, would you lead the tour of the facility?" *Why is she being nice to me?*

"Sure, follow me." We walk to the lobby. "We are planning to redesign this lobby." I explain the check-in desk will be handling the clients like a concierge would be giving our special clientele a little extra consideration. "Less waiting time in the lobby, more time in the massage room." They smile, and we continue room to room, until we reach room ten. "This is a special designed hot tub." I sigh. "But I am not sure what it does?" Everyone stares at me like I am a virgin Mary. "What?" "Brett didn't get a chance to show me how it works."

"I am so sorry to hear that." Detrick smirks with a European accent. "Let's all give it a test run." "Shall we?"

"Yes, I am game." Mamie dances. "Abby?"

"Sure, why not?" She turns to look at me. "You've got to get wet sometime." My heart races, face is flush with heat and I reluctantly nod turning on the hot tub.

We all get ready to get into the tub. As I undress behind the black tri-fold blind, I tremble, my heart is racing with excitement and fear. Abby and I are the first out from behind our blinds, nakedly we slide into the bubbling hot water across from each other. Then Detrick walks out strutting, like he is the hottest endowed man in town, (though he's not) and he slides into the hot tub on the left of Abby. Mamie pirouettes to the hot tubs edge and slides in on my right.

"Well, the water feels like one hundred four degrees to me." I sputter. "Shall I flip the switch." They nod. "Here we go." I push the big button on the side of the tub.

At first, I don't feel anything, but then a surge of hot water rushes between my legs; it feels like fingers touching my clit, sending heated tingles to my core. I moan uncontrollably, opening my eyes to see if anyone heard me and everyone has their eyes shut enjoying their own toying. I close my eyes enjoying the sensually tantalizing massage; my eminent orgasm is physically interrupted by many hands touching my hair, lips, breasts, buttocks and my intimate core.

"Breath…Darby." Mamie voice murmurs. "Let it come." I pant out a breath.

"Yes, release it." Abby sensually whispers in my ear. "I want to hear you." I groan with anticipation.

"Darby." Detrick breaths heated. "Tell me." "Darby."

"Oh my." "Oh-oh." I exhale as the tantalizing continues. "Don't stop!"

"Tell me more." He says stronger. "Darby."

"Yes!" I get louder verbally. "Don't stop." A set of warm lips kiss my breathless lips, another puts my left hand between her legs to touch her intimate core and Detrick takes my right hand to massage his hardened manhood. "Yes!" I yell passionately. He moans loudly; my right hand is caressing manhood harder and my left hand is creating a fire.

"Oh-oh!" "Dar-by." Mamie utters with desire. "Don't stop." Abby kisses my neck and turns to Mamie; she places Mamie's hand between the lips of her ladies' garden and begins to gasp passionately. We moan heatedly together. "Yes!" We orgasm in unison. My hot tub innocence is freed in our orge.

"You did marvelously, darling." Detrick utters catching his breath. "Abby, she is a natural."

"Yes, she is." Abby adds sarcastically. "Surprise-surprise." It feels good and I'm not afraid anymore. "No longer a hot tub virgin."

"Brett, would be proud of you, darling Darby." Mamie grimaces. "Now let's get this spa running." "Shall we?"

"Yes." I speak strongly. "Let's." I climb out of the hot tub naked to dress when Rachel walks into room ten wide-eyed with surprise

"Darby." Rachel stares at me. "What's going on in here?" "U-huh." I look at her innocently. "Oh, Rachel you're here." I stutter trying to hurry behind the blind. "I'll be with you in a moment."

"Yeah, I'll wait in your office." Rachel shuts the door, Abby turns off the tub motor, she walks behind her three-fold blind and I take a haggard deep breath of apprehension behind mine. *How do I explain this to my cousin? The truth?*

"Get dressed." I sigh stepping out from behind the blind. "We have a lot of work to do."

Mamie and Detrick get out of the hot tub and change into their clothes. Rachel is sitting on the sofa in my office when we walk inside; she straightens up as I walk behind my desk and smiles.

"Rachel, I know that you…" I begin to explain, but I stop. "Never mind, we need to start setting up the spa for business."

"Yes, we do." Abby pipes up. "Rachel, you can help me." "Darby." She tells. "Detrick and Mamie will help you with the lobby."

"Okay, Abby." I smile. "But if you need anything let me know." "Let's get to work." We all leave the office and start working.

A few hours later, the lobby is rearranged, new equipment is in place and in working order. It is a good thing, Abby took Rachel to set up the regular message rooms; if Rachel had seen what's in rooms seven through nine, she would freak out. Once the others arrive, Abby will help them set up the special clientele rooms and room ten.

"Rachel and Abby." I smirk. "We are hungry." I point at Detrick and Mamie. "Ready to go for dinner."

"Yes, starving." Abby concurs. "Rachel?"

"Yes, to food." Rachel says spiritedly. "Where?"

"At the hotel, of course." Detrick sputters sweetly. "My treat."

"Shall we walk over to the hotel?" Mamie asks gleefully. "Stretch out the legs."

"Yes, walking is fine with me." I smile and they all agree. "Great, let's go."

The conversation keeps to a minimum and the walk is quick to the hotel, the maître d' seats us in minutes and the food is served promptly. We eat and talk for a while; then Otis stops by the table with a smile, his eyes stare directly at Abby while he speaks to us.

"Darby, it is very nice to see you." Otis blurts out. "Where is Mr. Slade?"

"He is out of the country." I retort. "For a few months."

"Oh, I thought I saw him this morning." Otis stares confused. "Wasn't he here visiting you, Ms. Steed?"

I glare at Abby for an answer.

"Abby?" I plead. "Is that true?"

"Yes, Darby." She looks down at first, then at me. "Brett stopped by." Abby stops speaking for a moment. "He was worried about the special client list." Rachel gives Abby sneering glare.

"Special Clients." Otis repeats with concern. "What does that mean?"

"More money." Abby adds a sensual smile. "And business." "For the hotel and the spa." Otis smiles big and walks away; she leans over to me and whispers. "Brett is in love with you." "He warned me to behave."

"Oh-h." I smirk. "I-I."

"Don't worry." Abby touches my hand. "I am not getting in the way."

We finish eating in silence, I walk back to the spa with Rachel; she is staring at me, as I try to get in my car to go home.

"What, Rachel?" I blurt out. "I know you." "Say it."

"I'm not sure about what happened earlier in room ten." Rachel expresses. "I hope you know what you are doing." She walks away slowly to her car.

"Don't worry." I smile. "I can take care of myself."

"I hope so." Rachel expresses getting into her car.

I notice an envelope under my wipe blade on the front windshield, pull out from under the blade and open it. The note reads: "Beware of Detrick and Mamie, they are not whom they say. Diego." I sit still in my vehicle with the motor running, my heart is racing, and I can feel the fear of uncertainty creep up. *I wish Brett was here.* I put the note back in its envelope and drive home swiftly. The next four weeks goes by quickly, we stay busy setting up the spa for future business and Rachel joins us to help here and there. It is late evening when someone comes knocking on my front door, I make a mad dash from the kitchen; before I touch the handle of the front door, I smell men's cologne in my living room and I freeze. My heart is racing and fear creeps up.

"Who's there?" My low voice shakes. "I know you are in my house." I hiss. "Who is it?"

"It's Detrick." The figure whispers in the dark. "Don't answer the door." Detrick walks out of shadows.

"Why?" I whisper nervously. "And why are you here…in my house?"

"Please listen to me." Detrick says quietly. "I am not going to hurt you." "But the man outside your door, he is after me." He lightly touches my arm and guides me back to the kitchen. "Let him keep knocking, he'll leave soon." Detrick stands in the corner out of the way of the windows.

"Is he after to you?" I stare at him and he nods yes. "What did you do?" I grab the glass of iced tea off the counter. "I am sorry." "Where are my manners?" I smile trying not to be freaked out. "Would you like a glass of iced tea?"

"I don't think you really want to know, what…I did."

Detrick grumbles as I hold out the glass to him. "No tea." "Thanks." "What I did…it's not good." I glare upset.

"Do I need to call Brett?" I revel, with surety. "He'll know what to do."

"No, not-a-good idea." Detrick shakes his head. "He won't be happy."

"Why?" I inquire. "I don't understand."

"Because." He clears his knotted throat. "He'll kill me…for getting you involved."

"Involved?" I stare at him fearful. "How am I involved?" My voice shrills. "You showed up… at my house!"

"Darby, stop!" Detrick puts a hand out in the air, telling me to calm down, then his eyes hit the floor in a stare. "I-I never should have come to the Spa." Detrick mutters. "Or..." My stomach churns and I feel nauseous.

"If you don't want me to call Brett." I pipe up. "I am calling Abby."

"Yeah, Abby." He tries to smile. "She may be able to help us."

"Us?" My voice shrills louder. "I am not part of this Detrick." I grab the telephone receiver from the cradle and dial Abby's cell number. "Hey Abby, can you come over?" I sigh. "Detrick has gotten himself in trouble." "And he's trying to drag me into it." My hand shakes. "I-I understand, see you soon." I place the phone back on the cradle and stare at Detrick for a few seconds. "Abby will be here in twenty minutes."

I walk out of the kitchen to the living room and sit on the sofa, staring into the darkness. Not long after, Detrick comes in the living room taking the chair across from me. Twenty minutes feels like forever when you do not know what kind of danger you are in and what the outcome will be. Suddenly, a knock at the front door makes me leap from my seated position; I walk slowly the door to peak out the window and it is Abby standing there.

"Come in Abby." As I open the door quickly. "Please."

"Where is the ass?" Abby utters loudly.

"The ass is...here." Detrick seeps out of the darkness. "Abby."

"What the hell are you doing?" Abby scoops my arm and walks me to the sofa. "If Brett finds out you've mixed up Darby in this." Detrick covers his face with his hands. "He'll make you wish you didn't."

"I know." He rattles back. "I know." "I am sorry." His eyes meet mine. "Brett can't find out."

"O-kay." I am angry, wanting to scream at him. "But, I don't like it." Then seconds later the guilt of lying to someone I love dampens the rage. "And Detrick." "You." "Will…explain this issue to Brett when he returns." Abby smiles as I continue. "Do…you understand me?" I glare at him with no remorse and grab his arm strongly. "If not, I will tell him."

"No, no." His words stammer. "I'll do it."

Someone hammers on the door from outside with a heavy fist; screams words in a different language that I do not understand. Abby and Detrick stare at each other with surprise; then Abby grabs my arm and quickly walks me to my bedroom and sits down on my bed.

"Darby." She looks sincere. "One of Brett's bodyguards is outside." My eyes widen. "He'll want to speak with you." I nod shaken. "Tell him the truth." Abby sighs. "Or lie, no matter."

"Oh-h, okay."

She leaves me sitting there alone. The tears fill my eyes, my heart is racing, and I feel a knot tightening in my throat. I wipe the tears from my cheeks and walk to the front door brave-faced, ready to deal with whomever is outside my front door.

"Who is it?" I ask from inside.

"Miss Deel, it is Rudy." He says in a deep loud voice. "I work for Mr. Slade." I open the door slowly.

"How can I help you Rudy?" I smile.

"Ma'am, Mr. Slade requires your presence." Rudy smiles back. "So, he sent me to pick you up." *Just in the nick of time, I thought.*

"Oh, is he back?" I look inquiringly. "I thought he's still out of the country."

"Yes, he still is." Rudy clears his voice. "But he wants you to join him." A sigh of relief escapes me.

"Nice." I feel Abby's eyes on me from my bedroom doorway. "Shall I pack a few things before we leave?"

"Yes, that will be fine." Rudy smiles again. "I'll wait for you in the limo."

"Okay, I'll be out in a few minutes." I stare out at him walking away.

I shut the door, walking quickly into my bedroom, waltzing right pass Detrick and Abby without acknowledging them; then I get an overnight bag from my closet and start packing clothes in it.

"Darby, what are you doing?" Abby utters grabbing my arm tightly.

"I am going to see Brett." I glare at her and wrestle my arm loose from her grip. "Remember, you need to fix this." "Both of you." Detrick tries to speak but doesn't. "Abby take care of the spa until I return, please." I leave my bedroom, open the front door and leave them inside.

Rudy sees me coming outside, he gets out of the limo quickly to open my door; then he shuts it behind me. The limo smells like Brett's cologne and my heart races, I can't wait to see him. It seems like hours go by before we reach the airport, Rudy lowers the window between us as he slows down the limo.

"Miss Deel." Rudy states. "His jet will be landing in a few minutes."

"Thanks, Rudy." I smile brightly. "Can I ask you a question?"

"Sure, Miss Deel." His eyes smile back at me. "What would you like to know?"

"Do you know Brett's associates?" I inquire.

"Yes, I know some of them." He stares back. "Why?"

"I am wondering about Abby, Detrick and Mamie?"

I continue. "They seem…"

"Don't trust them." Rudy stares sternly into the rearview mirror and says clearly. "I don't, neither should you."

"Why?" I look lost. "Mr. Slade left me with them to set up the spa." I feel a little hurt.

"I understand your concern." He replies sincerely. "But, I think you should talk to Mr. Slade." Rudy turns away. "Miss Deel, his jet is parking."

Rudy gets out of the limo once again, he opens my door and helps me out; standing outside by the door of the limo as the airplane door opens. Brett lowers the stairs and takes two at a time to get to the ground; his smile lightens my heart, I smile, feeling the tears edging my eyes and we walk quickly toward each other. Brett's lips are warm on mine in our embrace, his arms engulf me, and I return the favor. I swing my arm out to slap him across the face, he stops me in mid-swat with his hand, tightens his grip around my waist with the other, his lips attack mine stealing my breath away; my resolve weakens, I relax in his embrace again and passionately kiss him back.

"Darby." Brett says breathless. "I missed you." He stares. "Why did you try to slap me?"

"We need to talk." His lips are less than an inch away. "I am mad at…" My voice is muffled by his kiss, I push back, and his breath tickles my neck. "Stop it." I giggle.

"Let's go, we can talk in the jet." He laughs. "It will be a few hours before we land again."

Brett swings me up in his arms and carries me into the jet. The plane takes off, after we are seated and buckled; once we reach flight level the seat belt sign turns off. I smile, Brett undoes his belt and mine, he takes my hand and leads me toward the back of the jet; his free hand opens a door to the sleeping quarters, he tosses me on the bed inside, shuts the door behind him and plops down beside me.

"Darby, have you made love in the air?" Brett snuggles in closer. I shake my head, no and I know I am about to ruin this moment, but…

"Why did you leave me with Abby at the spa?" I rattle out. "And who are Detrick and Mamie?" Brett backs away quickly, sitting up on the side of the mattress.

"Abby is there to help setup." Brett rubs his face with his hands. "Detrick and Mamie are sexual acquaintances, I met them through Abby." He looks at me unsure. "Why?"

"I am unsure about their intentions, especially Detrick's." I stammer. "He's acts recklessly."

"Did he hurt you?" My lips shimmy a little. "What happened?" Brett face heats up. "Tell me, Darby."

"No, he didn't hurt me." I didn't want to lie, so I skipped over the truth. "We all tried the hot tub, together." His face softens. "I liked it." I blush.

"Oh-h." "I wanted to try it out with you first." Brett sighs, moving in closer to me. "Alone." I my face lights up.

"We are alone, now." I stare at him seductively. "I think we can come up with something to keep us busy."

Brett and I move closer together, only separate by our clothes; which we slowly remove a garment with each kiss and touch, until naked; our bodies collide with fervor and heat, like waves in motion. As our climax nears its liquid release, sighing breathless moans of pleasure; he whispers: "I love you, Darby." We orgasm in blissful passion; I kiss him and whisper back. "I love you, too." We fall asleep wrap in a warm embrace, until the pilot announces we are landing in twenty minutes. Brett hands me my lacey bra and panties from the floor and smile sweetly; I stand up sliding my panties up my legs fully aware he is watching me intently and leaps to my rescue to hook the straps of my bra directly.

"Brett, I can do it myself." I sensually mutter. "I am a big girl."

"I know." He breaths on my neck. "But I-I." I look back at him and smile.

"We will be landing soon." I touch his hand. "You might want to get dressed."

"Yeah, it may be a good idea." Brett sits back to grab his pants and shirt. "We are meeting a few of the investors today."

"Oh-h…okay." I stare at him. "Where are we anyway?"

"Switzerland." He says, I laugh.

"What?" "I've never been here." I utter. "It's exciting."

"Great." His smile brightens. "I will show you around before our meeting."

"You want me at this meeting?" I inquire. "I'm not sure if I'd be any help."

"Yes, I do." Brett stands up to pull up his slacks. "I wasn't sure the investors were keen to it." Brett continues. "But, yesterday they called and want to meet you as well." I look at him intently. "Besides, I didn't want to leave you at home." The pilot makes another announcement, we are landing. "We need to get in our seats, Darby." Brett finishes tucking in his dress shirt into his slacks, takes my hand and walk outside the room together. We sit in the seats and buckle up our belts for landing.

Once we land and the door opens, I step outside to a breath-taking view of a mountain side and a small village off in the distance. Brett holds my hand as we walk down the stairs off the jet; then his hand releases mine and slides across the small of my back, holding me against his side.

"Darby, you are so beautiful." His lips swipe my forehead. "The meeting starts in three hours in Zurich." Brett smirks. "We have a few hours to tour the cities on the way to Zurich." I nod. "Let's get going."

The driver opens the door to the limo and we climb inside. Brett tells the driver where to go and we leave the private air strip. The first stop is an old museum of German architecture in the Jura Hills, then the we stopped in Lucern for lunch at quaint Inn and our last stop is an hour away in Zurich. I rest my head against Brett's chest to relax, his breath breezes against my cheek and I fall asleep; he leans his head against the seat and falls asleep too.

Back at home, Abby and Detrick start contacting prospective clients for the spa; Mamie is a computer programmer by trade, she busies herself with updating the scheduling parameters for regular clients and the elite clients. They work together to get everything set for a re-grand opening in four weeks.

"Hello." My cellphone rings waking me out of a sound sleep. "Who is this?"

"Darby, it's Abby." She snickers. "Are you okay?"

"Yeah, you woke me up." I stretch my arms and sit up slowly not to wake up Brett. "What's going on?"

"I had a nice conversation with Otis at the hotel over dinner last night." Abby states. "He thinks that it would be a great idea if we rename the spa."

"Really?" I cross my legs on the seat next to Brett. "Oh yeah, Brett was talking about that before the remodel." I grab a cold bottle of water from the side cubby. "Do you have any names?"

"Well, Otis and I were wondering if you'd like to name the spa "Allure Me." Abby sparks. "He thinks it is catchy."

"That's, "Allure Me, right?" I ask.

"It means physical attractiveness." Abby adds.

"It is definitely appropriate." I giggle softly. "And it fits the spa." Brett opens his eyes and smiles at me. "Hey Ba-be." I blush. "Abby's on the phone."

"Is everything okay?" He leans over to me kissing my cheek. "Good morning, beautiful."

"Yes." "Abby and Otis had a conversation at the hotel." Brett nods, I continue. "They think we should rename the Spa, "Allure Me." He smiles reaching his hand out form my cellphone; I give it to him, his hand brushes mine sending tingles to my brain.

"Abby, the name is perfect." "How is the remodel going?" Brett laughs. "Great, are we set for a re-grand opening?" His hand slides into mine, holding it lightly. "Okay, we will be heading back to Big Bay in a few days." "Bye." Brett disconnects the call and leans over to me to place the phone on the other side of my body; his eyes are gorgeous green with flecks of golden hazel, staring at me. We are face to face when his lips launch into mine, warm and strong. "Babe, huh." Brett grimaces. "I love you."

"Yeah, you let it slip last night." I am breathless and return with a passionate kiss; his body pushes me back against bottom cushion and releasing my crossed legs placing his body between them. "I love you, too."

The driver calls us through the intercom and announces will be arriving at the destination in five minutes; we quickly sit up and smoothing ourselves out. I fix my makeup and he straightens his tie. A few seconds before I put on my lipstick, he turns to me and kisses me; then his arms take me in closer for deeper kisses.

"Brett, we can't." I push him away. "Remember, the meeting." I touch his cheek, he pouts.

The limo stops out in front of the Bank of Zurich, we exit the vehicle, enter the high-status establishment and go through security for clearance; we get on the elevator to the seventeenth-floor conference room for the investor meeting. After a few hours, we leave a successful meeting and head back to the private airport to fly to our next investors meeting; Brett and I sleep most of the flight on the jet to Rome, Italy. We walk the city streets after an Italian breakfast at a small café before the meeting; Brett and I stop to look in a small chapel; we stay to watch a simple Italian wedding in progress.

"This is a beautiful little church." I whisper, he takes my hand in his and smiles. "So quaint and comfy."

"I think." He breaths. "I could get married here." My heart leaps and beats harder. "What do you think?"

"Yes, I-I." His face frowns.

"Darby, I'm not asking you to marry me." Brett mumbles upset. "I only wanted to know what I thought." I feel the tears welling-up and I get up quickly dashing out the door, Brett is not far behind.

"Darby!" Brett hollers to me outside. "Darby!" "Please stop." He grabs my arm.

"You are an intolerable jerk!" I yell. "How can you say that you love me?" I rattle on angrily. "You're a twisted freak." I yank my arm loose walking to the limo standing by, I get inside and scoot myself to the far side of the seat. Brett climbs inside shortly after and stays next to the door.

We sit in silence to the Bank of Italy and barely make eye contact; the meeting goes well; the investors are set, the trip to the airplane is quick. The jet takes off, his hand brushes mine, I slide it away from him and he grabs it tightly.

"Don't Darby." Brett hand-shakes as it lightens its grip. "I am… so sorry." "I didn't mean to hurt you."

"I am a jerk." He carries on. "I've been alone for a long time." "I know it's not a good excuse." "But…" The tears escape his eyes, he wipes them away fast and straightens his position; the seat belt sign turns off, undo my seat belt, climb into his lap and kiss him. "Darby, no." I kiss him again and he returns the favor.

"Brett, I love you." I say sincerely. "I want this relationship to work." "But..."

"I want to be with you too, only you." Brett touches my cheek. "I have some inner demons, that I need to work out." His eyes shine. "Please be patient."

"Okay." "I'll try." I smile. "How long is this flight?"

"We will be back tomorrow afternoon." He says, I curl up closer to him and kiss him passionately.

"Talk to me." I plead and sigh. "Or I can think of something that would occupy our time."

"You're a minx." Brett stands up with me in his arms, carries me to the bedroom and we stretch out on the bed. "I love you, Darby." I start unbuttoning his dress shirt and tug him over to me by his tie.

"Shut up and kiss me, Brett." I growl.

"Your wish is my command." He spouts sweetly.

Meanwhile at the Allure Me, Abby starts scheduling hotel guest and special clients for the week of re-grand opening with Sasha the cheeky hotel concierge. Unfortunately, Otis is a little put off that Abby didn't ask him to help with scheduling; he is very intrigued and wants to get to know Abby better. As for Detrick and Mamie; they left the country, the fiasco with his bookie started causing problems with Allure Me business and Brett insisted they disappear for a while. My cousin Rachel has been calling and leaving messages for me but flying around Europe isn't helping our connection. Once the jet hit American air space, my cellphone goes crazy pining messages and missed calls; the noise wakes us out of sleep and I get up to look at it.

"Oh, wow." I yawn. "How long before we land?

"I don't know." Brett says stretching out on the bed. "A few hours, I guess." "Come back to bed."

"Rachel has left me several messages." I grab his shirt and my panties off the floor. "I'll be back soon."

Brett has already fallen back to sleep as I walk into the other room. "Rachel, what's wrong?"

"Thanks for calling back finally." She grumbles. "I've been worried about you." "Something isn't right about the Spa."

"What happened?" I sigh. "Abby has everything under control."

"That's just it." "Why is Abby in charge?" Rachel yawns. "It is your business."

"True." "And she is not in charge." I sit in a comfy chair. "But Brett wanted me to go with him to the investors meetings." I explain. "So, I left her in charge of setup and scheduling until I return."

"When do you come home?" Rachel sputters.

"Today, in few hours." The plane drops altitude suddenly and the seat belt light comes on. "Or sooner." "I'll call you back something is up with the jet."

"What?" "What?" Rachel's voice gets louder and the call drops, I turn my phone off Brett is out of the sleeping quarters in seconds pulling up his pants.

"Put on your seat belt Darby." Brett says sternly charging toward the cock pit. "Pilot, what's going on?" The jet starts to level out a few minutes later.

"Brett!" I holler. "Is everything okay?"

"Yes." Brett and the pilot walk out of the cock pit. "Jake said they hit a major air pocket." The handsome pilot nods. "The co-pilot is diverting us around the storm clouds." The pilot walks back into the cock pit. "Thanks, Jake."

“Now, how long will it be before we land?” I ask.

“Still only a few hours.” He sighs. “Why?” Brett eyebrows frown. “Is something wrong at home?”

“Well, it’s not fair to leave Abby with everything.”

“Plus, I miss working.” Brett leans in for a kiss. “A little.”

“Mm-mm, I miss you already.” His lips are warmly inviting. “Let’s go back to bed.” “I need to snuggle.”

“Okay, snuggling it is.” He helps me out of my chair and we return to our sleeping quarters.

The next few hours go by quickly; Brett and I are showered, dressed and ready to disembark the jet. Abby arrives in the limo, they park next to the jet and wait for us disembark. We enter the vehicle minutes later, Abby greets us as we promptly drive to the newly innovated spa. It didn’t faze me until we reach the parking lot of the spa, that the new driveway is now connected directly with the hotel, the sign reads ‘Allure Me’ is on the building and the outside is repainted too. My eyes tear up upon exiting the limo and I smile.

“Wow, I am floored.” I look at them simultaneously. “Abby.” I gasp. “Brett.” “It looks amazing.”

“Wait until you see the inside.” Abby says gleefully. “You’ll love it.”

“Ladies, let’s go.” Brett ushers us forward and steps ahead to open the door. “Darby.” “Abby.”

“Thanks Brett.” Abby says sarcastically. “Such a gentleman.”

“Thank you, Brett.” I take his hand. “Let’s check out our new digs.”

"Okay babe." Brett whispers softly and it sends warm tingles to my heart.

"Darby and Brett." "What so you think of the new reception area?" Abby dashes out with a beaming smile. "Mamie had the computer already programmed before she left with Detrick." She smirks. "I booked it with clients for the re-grand opening."

"Abby, it looks amazing." My heart dances. "The desk set up is perfect."

"You did well, Abby." Brett supplies. "Show us the rooms." His eyes sparkle. "All the rooms."

"Okay." Abby smiles. "Follow me." We walk behind Abby to each room one by one, viewing its contents, stopping at the room with no door. "Now there has been a change in this room." "I hope you both like it." She slowly opens the large black curtains, simultaneously Brett's hand slowly slides down my spine to my lower back resting on my backside.

"Wow, it is..." I couldn't get the words out as the tingles vibrate through my core from his touch.

"Yeah, Abby." Brett is exhilarated. "Wow, it is perfect."

"Sensual, sexy and mind-blowing." I utter the words out softly. "Abby, you used the storage room." Staring at the new opening, I continue walking into room eleven. "It is double-tabled massage room for couples."

"That's correct." Abby supplies, I laugh. "I have the construction crew coming to install a new double door."

"But Abby, where is the storage room?" I ask.

"Darby, when you bought this place." I listen intently. "They didn't tell you about the extra room behind the wall to the basement." Abby opens the door. "See." My eyes widen. "The movers found it accidently." "One of the old massage table edges poked a big hole in the wall on the way to the basement." "So, I had the contractor open the wall and extend the floor to the basement stairs."

"Wow." "Who knew what was hiding behind that wall, room number twelve." I laugh. Abby and Brett smile.

"Now, I have another surprise." I listen. "I had the office remodeled too."

"You did?" "Why?" Abby throws the office door open, I gasp. "Wow." I place my hands to my face in awe. "It is amazing." Where the sofa sat is a new slim designed massage table and water bath resides next to it on top of a small chest of drawers.

"Brett." Abby smiles at him turning to leave. "I'll let you show Darby around her new office." She closes the door behind her, he locks it and takes off his suit jacket.

"Brett what's going on?" I stare at him with a curious smile.

"No worries, darling." Brett says seductively. "It will be my pleasure to show you."

"Brett, what?" His left eyebrow raises up and he smirks unbuttoning his dress shirt.

"It is time to wake you up." Brett quickly pulls me close. "I plan to educate you fully." I release the button to his slacks, dropping the garment to the floor.

"Oh-h, my teacher." I breathe. "I presume." I pull him even closer. "But, I think I will prove to be an excellent student." I kiss his sultry lips. "Or you may be the one who learns something new."

"Teacher's pet." He drizzles. "I-I." I stop him with another heated kiss.

"Stop thinking." I whisper. "Kiss me." The phone rings several times, starling us back into reality. I reluctantly answer it. "Thank you for calling Allure Me, this is Darby."

The man speaks quick and I stare at Brett. "U-huh, I understand." My look scares Brett at first. "Yes, I will talk to Mr. Slade about this issue." Brett slowly pulls up his pants and buttons his shirt. "Thank you for calling, bye."

"What is it Darby?" Brett's grimace turns to a frown.

"Oh-h, Brett." I utter loudly. "I think we have a big problem."

"What?" He looks even more irate. "What is it Darby?"

"Well, Detrick and Mamie were arrested in New York trying to leave the country." I step back from Brett. "But before the FBI and CIA were involved." He stares unhinged, putting his fingers through his thick dark hair on his head. "Mamie threw you and Abby under the bus regarding the business you've been in together for years."

"Oh fuck, go get Abby." Brett's face turns from calm to fearful. "And I need to call the investors." I walk quickly out the office to find Abby in the lobby.

"Abby." I breath heavily. "Brett needs to speak to you right away." She is staring outside at the red and blue flashing lights of the Police cars surrounding the Spa. "Oh shit, what's happening now?"

"Go to Brett." Abby states clearly. "You'll need to find a way out."

I run to the office, Brett is sitting on the sofa with his phone snuggly to his ear speaking in a foreign language. Once his conversation is complete Brett stands up promptly and begins to pace around the office, not looking at me.

"Brett, what's going on?" I calmly grab his arm stopping him from pacing. "The Police are here, why?" I touch his face tenderly making him look at me. "Are we in trouble?" I ask sincerely. "You need to talk to me." His body sways back and forth.

"No, I need to get you out of here." Brett's arms wrap around me tightly like a glove. "I want you to be safe." He pulls the cellphone out of his pocket again. "Rudy." His chest heaves. "You need to get Darby out of here." Brett listens to Rudy talk and smiles.

"Keep her safe." "Thank you, my friend." I look at Brett, my face feels flush and my palms are sweaty.

"Rudy, can get you to a safe place." He holds my hands gently. "He will protect you until this fiasco is over." I launch into him, squeezing him in a tight hug and kiss him swiftly. "Go out the back door." He says with a fake smile. "Rudy will be there in the limo."

"Brett wait, wait." I smile. "I-I."

"Darby, go quickly." Brett eyes shimmer. "I know." "I love you, too."

"But, I." I try to add.

"Darby, they are coming in the building." "You need to leave now." He pushes me out the door of the office. "Hurry."

I run quickly down the basement stairs to the back door; the limo is waiting outside, I get inside it fast and Rudy opens the window between us.

"Miss Darby." Rudy turns his body sideways. "On your left, grab the top of the seatbelt." I grasp it. "Now, push it into the fastener." I do it and it clicks. "Good." "Now, yank it toward you." I pull it, a secret compartment opens in the seat below, under the window where Rudy sits. "Quickly get inside." Rudy adds. "The Police are coming." I slide inside, the lid shuts automatically, I feel trapped in the dark at first.

"Get out of the limo, now!" The Policeman yells at Rudy. "With your hands up!"

"Search the vehicle." The Officer in charge speaks up. "Make sure you toss it." "Panels and all."

"Yes Sir." The young Policeman utters.

I wait, for what seems like hours inside the hidden compartment, while the Policemen made a lot of noise searching the limo. Finally, they are finished. Rudy is allowed back in his vehicle, but first he starts putting the panels back on the inside of the doors of the limo. He hears the police cars pull away and smile.

"Miss Darby, are you okay?" Rudy asks.

"Yes." I announce.

"Good." He continues. "I will let you out soon." "We have to get to the safe house first, okay?"

"Okay, but." I start to say.

"Sorry, it won't be a long ride." I hear him get out of the limo compartment and enter the driver's area. "I promise, Darby." Rudy continues. "It won't be long."

I couldn't tell if we are going East or West, North or South at first, but I knew we were going outside of Big Bay Lake. Until we drove over a long bumpy road a few minutes later, we were headed toward Bumford going South on Route Ten. I thought there isn't anything out that way except for cabins, an old vacant dilapidated hotel and Big Buck Lake. When the bumps ended, I start counting Mississippi's as we drive towards where ever, like I did as a child with my friends heading to the lake or cabins. Not long after, Rudy stop the vehicle, he gets out and releases me from my hiding spot inside the limo.

"Are you okay, Miss Darby?" He asks.

"Yes, Rudy." I climb outside the limo and look around. The area seems familiar, I realize he brought me to my family's old cabin in the woods. "Why did you bring me here?"

"Mr. Slade said you would be safe here." I stare at him.

"How did he know about this place and the cabin?"

I ask kindly. "I never told him about my past."

"Mr. Slade knows everything, Miss." Rudy looks a little startled. "Let's go inside." "I'll start a fire."

We walk inside the cabin together, it almost looks the same as when I was child, but there are new boards on the floor and ceiling. The walls have been recently painted and new furniture in place of the old. Rudy goes directly to the fireplace, cleans the flute, stocks the wood on the rack and starts the fire. I walk into the kitchen with a smile, I remember my mother cooking food for all of us and humming her favorite song. I return to the living room, sit next where Rudy sat watching the fire and smiling.

"I remember my time here." I begin to tell Rudy my story. "My parents died when I was twelve, my older sister Mable took care of me until I was eighteen and my two other siblings were off to college and the military." I sigh, sadden a little and smile. "Now, I am the only one alive out of a family of six; Wade died in a housefire, Andrew was killed in action in Afghanistan and Mabel passed away a few years ago from Cancer."

"Wow, it's like you and Brett are same." Rudy adds.

"What do you mean?" I reach out.

"He's alone too." Rudy answers. "Two souls lost and now found." His eyes sparkle in the firelight.

"Brett never talks about his family." I stare out. "I thought they were estranged, not gone."

"No, he is orphan." Rudy grimaces. "You'd think he came from old money."

"What about Will?" I ask. "He is Brett's brother."

"No." "Will was adopted by the Slade's, too." Rudy adds. "Brett built his business from the ground up and no one to share it with." His voice wavers. "Until you…" Rudy looks at me. "He's a good man." "Don't give up on him." I smile.

"Are you hungry, Rudy?" I ask. "I am starving."

"Yes, Miss." He smiles. "I'll see what I can find." Rudy stands up. "Stay inside, you'll be safe out here." He leaves the cabin and drives away in the limo. My cellphone vibrates a few minutes later.

"Hello." The reception makes a crackling noise. "Who is it?"

"Darby." Brett's voice fades in and out. "Can you hear me?"

"Yes, but the reception is bad out here." I spout. "What's up?"

"Is Rudy with you?" He asks.

"No, Rudy went to get us something to eat." My face frowns. "Why?" What's wrong?" Brett is quiet.

"Brett, are you still there?"

"Yes." "But…" The call connection is lost. My heart beats faster.

"Brett." "Brett." I try to redial his number and it won't go connect; now I am scared that Rudy won't be back. I need to protect myself.

If my memory serves me, there is a secret cubby in the kitchen where my father kept his shotgun; it is time to get it out of hiding, I walk slowly into the darkened kitchen trying to recall the hiding place. I remember there was a sticker that was placed many years ago on the board covering it, it pops into view; I slide the old board away and the shotgun and bullets sit inside, still waiting for someone to retrieve them. I clean the weapon, taking care that it has been years since it was loaded and used, this was something my father taught me how to do at young age. I hear noises from outside the front door, I hope it is Rudy and not someone else. I carry the shotgun with me to look outside; I sigh, Rudy is unloading the groceries from a different vehicle and coming inside cursing up a storm.

"Shit." Rudy looks up. "Sorry, Darby." "I had to get another vehicle." He explains walking with bags into the kitchen. "Brett called me." "And said that he has to leave the country again." My eyes-widen in surprise. "But, not to worry." "He'll be back to you soon." Places them down on the table in a heap.

"Why did he have to leave?" I plead.

"Abby isn't in trouble." Rudy utters. "Otis covered for her, she was released. "But, Detrick and Mamie are creating problems for Brett with the investors." He starts unpacking one of the grocery bags. "So, he's meeting with the investors to calm them down."

"Oh-h wow, Otis saved Abby from jail." I laugh. "He is really smitten with her." "Where are Detrick and Mamie?"

"Interpol has them now." Rudy smirks. "I told you they were trouble."

"Good, what's for dinner?" As I unpack a grocery bag too.

"I am going to make my Mama's specialty." Rudy glimmers. "So, sit down by the fire and I will call you when it is ready." He adds. "By the way, is there a generator for this place?"

"Yes, it is in the shed." I point outside the kitchen window.

"Great, I will go get it running."

Rudy dashes out the back door. I leave the kitchen and sit on the sofa by the fire in the living room. Soon, the lights flickered on, Rudy is in the kitchen cooking up a storm and the smell coming from the kitchen is making my stomach growl with hunger.

“Mm-m, it smells so good in here.” I stroll into the kitchen, Rudy has my Mama’s old apron wrapped around his rather large waist. I giggle, and he smiles.

“You like it.” He models it femalely with his hands on his hips. “I bet your Mama never looked so good.”

“I can say that’s true.” I laugh out. “I am starving, is it ready.”

“Yes.” His voice sings. “Can you grab some plates?

I hand him two plates, he scoops out large spoons full of food on to the plates; I pull out forks and napkins, while he places plates on the table by the fire.

“Rudy, the food looks great and it smells amazing.” I hand him a fork and napkin. “What is it?”

“My Mama’s special concoction.” Rudy sighs with a smile. “She used to make it when I was young.” I taste it and smile.

“Wow, this is wonderful.” I take another bite. “It has a Cajun flavor to it.” “It is very good.”

“Would you like a drink?” Rudy adds. “I bought wine, whiskey and tequila.” He stands.

“Yes, a glass of tequila.” I smile, hoping it will calm my nerves. “Would be great.” “Thank you.” Rudy walks back into the kitchen, a few seconds later he returns with the bottle and two glasses.

“Do you need any ice?” He asks.

“No.” I grab the tequila bottle and pour it into the glasses. “Here you go.” I place my hand on his as he reaches for the glass. “Now, are you really going to tell me what’s going on?” I give him a serious stare.

“Mr. Slade should be…” He sighs deeply. “Okay, I’ll tell you what I know.” His hand pulls away from mine. “But, the rest is up to Mr. Slade.” I nod.

Rudy starts talking, he begins when Brett hired him ten years ago in New York City; he only had arrived three days earlier from Moldova in Eastern Europe looking for work and a new place to call home.

"Mr. Slade noticed me standing in line at the employment office of a limo agency." His eyes sparkle. "He asked me if I would be his driver." "I agreed with a nod." He shifts his leg and let out a sigh. "That's when he realized I spoke very little English." "Mr. Slade made it his mission to teach me." The firelight begins to get low, Rudy gets up to add more wood to the fire; he continues the story while he loads the fireplace. "I found out Mr. Slade also spoke Romanian, my home language." Rudy grimaces and returns to his former seat. "We quickly became friends and confidants." Rudy picks up his glass and swallows the tequila in it. "His work is very important to him." He swiftly puts the glass down and pours more tequila in it. "He has adversaries from all walks of life." His voices shrill. "Some from legal deals." He picks up the glass once again. "Some from illegal deals." "That's were Mamie and Detrick came in the picture." The glass is empty again and places it on the table, he is about to refill it again when I put my hand over the top of the glass.

"Please finish telling me the story." I say realizing if he drank anymore he wouldn't continue. "I need to know what's happening." Rudy relaxes against the back of the sofa.

"Mamie and Detrick were working for a mobster in Russia." "Once Mr. Slade employed them, his business became the mobster's business without his knowledge." He scratches his head. "Mr. Slade didn't find this out until a few months later." "When his investment business grew tremendously, clients were coming out of the blue." "He realized it wasn't from legit business, but illegal ones." "So, he cut off most of those contacts and stopped dealing with them." "One of those clients, Diego Fortuna is trying to destroy his business and reputation." "We think he is Detrick's real boss from the Italian Mafia." Rudy kicks his feet up on the table to relax more. "Okay." He yawns.

"When did Abby get involved with Brett?" I ask.

"Abby was already working with Mr. Slade at this time." He stares at me. "I think she was involved with him too." I sigh, knowing what he says was true. "But, Mr. Slade wouldn't allow her to get close to him." "He's very protective of his heart." His voice crackles, grabbing his glass and fills it up with tequila. "This is last one, promise." "I'll drink it slow." I nod. "He told me once, that he had been in love; but the woman was crazy." My eyes widen with interest. "She tried to kill him." Rudy's head drops a little. "But instead she blew up his family's house with his parents, some of his siblings and herself in it."

"What?" I gasp. "Oh my, that's why he…"

"He gets distant and cold." Rudy smiles at me. "But he loves you and I haven't seen him this happy in a while." "That's why I told you to give him time, he's a good man." He rubs his eyes with his hands. "Now, I need to rest Darby." "The bedroom is yours and I'll sleep here, okay."

"Yes." "Thank you, Rudy." I yawn and stretch. "I am getting tired."

I walk slowly to my parents' old room that's been remodeled; it has a new four-post bed, dressers and new paint on the walls. While I pull back the blanket and climb in bed, I feel a little sad because it makes me miss them and all the happiness we felt here as a family. I lay still, scared wondering what's happening to him, hoping I will see him again. I shut my eyes wishing Brett is here holding me, until I fall asleep. In the morning, I wake up and Rudy is gone; he left a note on the counter and a pot of coffee on the stove in the kitchen. It read: "Be back soon, checking in with Mr. Slade and picking up more supplies. We may be here for a while. Rudy." I sigh, pouring myself a cup of coffee, that's still hot; so, Rudy didn't leave that long ago. I look outside the kitchen window, the bright morning light peers over the large pine trees lining Big Buck Lake, it is going to be a beautiful day. *Maybe, I'll take a stroll around the lake. I thought.* I pour cereal in a bowl with milk and eat it. Soon, I finish my second cup of coffee and wash my dishes. Rudy still hasn't returned, I decide it is time to take walk outside by the lake. The breeze from the lake is relaxing, I remember were the path was when my friends use to come to the lake with us; I follow it around the lake, until I reach the old not so vacant hotel. There are people moving stuff out of the structure and bringing new equipment inside it, I over hear one of the foreign men talking in a language I didn't understand to another who yells at him to speak English. The male worker calls him Patrova, they mention Big Bay Hotel, Allure Me spa and Mr. Slade in not so nice context; so, I quietly leave the location making my way back to the cabin unnoticed and see that Rudy has returned.

"Darby, where have you been?" Rudy gets loud. "I told you not to leave the cabin."

"I know, I'm sorry." I utter. "I felt cooped up so, I took a walk."

"I almost called Mr. Slade." He growls.

"Rudy, listen to me." Rudy stand still. "When I was walking by the old vacant hotel." His eyes are fixed on me. "It wasn't vacant, there are men moving stuff in and out of the building." "They speak a foreign language, I don't understand." Rudy moans. "But one yelled at them to speak English." "Also, I overheard them discussing the Big Bay Hotel, the Allure Me and Mr. Slade." "It wasn't very cordial."

"I will inform Mr. Slade." Rudy states firmly. "And you need to stay inside the cabin, please."

"Okay, I will." I walk inside and sit on the sofa.

"I brought you a Nintendo DS to play games on." He hands it to me. "I know it isn't much but, it will keep you occupied."

"Thanks." "How is Brett?" I ask. "Is he okay?"

"He is doing okay." Rudy smiles. "Mr. Slade flew into New York last night from Italy." Rudy looks back to me as he stands up. "He misses you, too." Then walks back to the door, he holds the shotgun by the door up in the air. "Listen, I want you to have the shotgun loaded and ready to use." "Just in case, you need it." I nod "Be back soon, please stay inside." The door shuts behind him and I am alone again.

I turn on the Nintendo DS to play a few games, add wood to the fireplace and relax on the sofa. After a while, I decide to make dinner for Rudy and me; I pick a few items out of the refrigerator, start the pilot on the gas stove and begin cutting meat and vegetables. I pull out the cast iron pan and put the cut-up meat in the pan to cook, stir in the vegetables, add some of the wine, stirring slowly to simmer and put the lid on it.

Suddenly, I hear people talking from outside the cabin near the lake, the voices are moving closer to my vicinity; I can feel the hair standing up on my neck, I grab the loaded shotgun near me and cock-it ready to fire. I peek out the window and I see three of the men from the old hotel on the lake; they are walking slowly toward my cabin armed with guns, chatting back and forth to one another. The closer they get, the more nervous I become; until Rudy pulls up in the driveway of the cabin. He walks toward them, unlocking the safety on his nine-millimeter next to his hip.

"Hey gentlemen." Rudy announces. "Can I help you?" They smile at him.

"No, no." The tall guy says in reply. "We're taking walk around the lake." "My name is Wilhem Patrova." "And these are my sons." "Mikela and Nicola." I'm still watching them from the window with the shotgun in hand.

"Nice to make your acquaintance." Rudy reaches out his hand. "My name is Rudy Caswell." "My sister Darby is inside making dinner." "Would you like to join us?"

"No, thank you." Wilhem waves his brothers back toward the old hotel. "We need to get back to work." "It was nice to meet you."

"You as well." Rudy waves as they walk away; he walks quickly inside the cabin. "Darby, pack up your stuff." He rushes out. "We need to leave now."

"Who are they?" He shakes his head, side to side. "Okay, but we need to eat this first." I smile. "I am starving." He sits down quickly, scoffing down the food on his plate and smiles.

"This-this is very good." Rudy says with a mouthful of food. "Can I have more, please?"

"Sure." Handing him the large spoon. "Take as much as you want." He starts scooping out a large portion from the cast iron pan, smiling brightly, then stops suddenly

"Did you want more too?" I laugh.

"No." I touch his hand. "You go ahead and eat it."

"I will wash the dishes, pack up the kitchen and turn off the generator." Rudy talks in between bites. "You pack up the bedroom, put out the fireplace and meet me in the car."

"Oh okay." Look at him confused. "But, where will we go?"

"No worries." He declares. "Mr. Slade has several places we can stay." I sigh.

A few hours later, it is almost midnight when we enter a large apartment, a hundred miles from Big Bay Lake; it has two large bedrooms, a huge kitchen and living room. Rudy and I carry the packed items into the dwelling, including the shotgun and bullets.

"Darby, welcome home for now." Rudy says sleepy. "I am off to bed."

"Yes, I am too." "Rudy, can I use your phone to call Brett?" I grumble. "I left mine at the spa days ago."

"Yeah, sure." He hands it to me before leaving the room. "Put it on the charger before you go to sleep."

"I will." "Thank you." Rudy walks away to the room on the left. I dial Brett's number. It rings twice before it is answered. "Hello, Brett."

"Darby, it's nice to hear your voice." Brett sounds great. "Are you okay?"

"Yes, Rudy has been wonderful." I stall a little. "I miss you." "When can I see you?"

"I know." "I miss you too." His voice wavers. "I don't know when it will be safe, but I will find a way." A crackling noise crosses over the phone and our connection is lost.

"Brett, are you there." "Brett." I sigh sadly and plug Rudy's phone into the charger on the kitchen counter.

I walk to bedroom next to the kitchen, the room is decorated nicely with powder blue walls, is very soothing; I yawn smiling at the four-post bed calling to me 'it's time to go to sleep my dear, crawl into my comfort', of course I listen and fall asleep quickly.

In the morning, I wake to a very loud thumping noise like someone is being thrown up against the wall; my first reaction is to find out what's going, but next thought is to hide quickly. I survey the room and spot a chaffer robe in the corner, big enough for me to climb inside. There are clothes still hanging inside, so I push them aside and crawl in, as I shut the door from inside someone enters the room. I swiftly move the clothes in front of me to stay hidden; my heart feels like it is racing out of my chest as the person or persons walk near the chaffer robe, speaking the same foreign language I heard at the lake by the old hotel. I wait inside my hiding place until I do not hear them anymore, I am about to open the door when I hear Rudy barely calling out my name. I quickly push the doors open hoping to find that my bodyguard isn't dead. I rush over to Rudy's body slummed against the doorway of the bedroom, he is not moving.

"Rudy." "Rudy!" I speak louder. "Answer me." "Rudy, please!" He moves a little, trying to speak.

"I-I." Rudy mumbles. "Need my phone."

"Okay." I yank it off the charge and turn it on.

He pressed a few buttons. I grab a dishtowel from the counter to apply pressure to the gaping hole in his stomach.

"I need Ramsey, boss." I can hear Brett saying okay and Rudy hands me the phone.

"Brett, he needs help." I am distraught. "I can't stop the bleeding."

"It's okay." "Ramsey is coming." Brett say trying to calm me down. "He will take care of Rudy." "I am sending Otis to get you." "He will take you to my house."

"Okay." I cry. "I-I."

"I know you're scared." He sighs. Rudy let out his last breath and dies in front of me.

"Rudy's dead." The tears flow down my cheeks. "I need you."

"I will see you soon." Brett supplies. "Ramsey is there." "Go outside." "Otis will be there soon."

"Will you stay on the phone with me?" I sniff and wipe my tearful face. "Until Otis picks me up."

"I will." I hear crackling on his end of the connection. "But, if we lose the signal." "Remember I love you." I walk down the flight of stairs to the first floor and walk outside the building. Otis pulls up in his gray Mercedes Benz, smiling.

"Brett, he is here." I hear nothing. "Brett, are you there?" No reply. I get inside Otis's car and we leave.

"Darby, are you hurt?" He sees the blood on my hands and shirt.

"No, it's not mine." I look out the door window. "I don't want to talk about it, right now." Otis nods. "Can you take me home to pick up clothes before you bring me to Brett's house?"

"Sure." He smiles trying to avoid the conversation about my overall condition. "But, Mr. Slade insist that I take you to his place straightway."

"Oh, he insists, does he." I feel anger welling up inside me. "Otis, please take me home." "First."

I breath out. "Then, I will go willingly to his house."

"Okay." Otis looks like he might die of anxiety. "I hope Mr. Slade."

"I am not worry about Mr. Slade, Otis." He continues to drive us back to Big Bay Lakes in silence. When we reach my house, stare at its burnt structure and cry with unbelief. "Who burn down my house?" I utter in between sobs.

"I don't know." Otis says nervous. "But, I need to get you to a safe place." He declares strongly.

"Mr. Slade's?" He doesn't say anything. "Otis, where are you taking me?"

"A very safe place." I cover my face with my hands. "It is a long drive, but I know no one will find you."

"You will tell Mr. Slade, right." I stare at him. "Where you are taking me?"

"Yes." Otis wipes his forehead with a hanky from his suit jacket. "When it is safe for you."

Otis has been a friend of my family since before I was born, so I know I can trust him. Relaxing back against the seat, fall asleep for a while only to wake up to an empty car and Otis is nowhere to be found. Quickly I sit up, he parked the car in old gas station lot; so, decide to get out of the car when Otis appears from the side of the rundown building, he waves at me.

"The plumbing still works in this rundown heap." Otis announces kindly. "You may want to use the facility before we leave." I smile and points to where he came from. "It right over there." "I'll wait in the car for you." I walk around the building, enter the restroom and Rudy's phone rings.

"Hello." The phone crackles a little.

"Darby, where are you?" Brett states. "You're not at my house."

"I know." "Otis is taking me somewhere safe." My hands are shaking, as I try to unbutton my jeans. "Someone burnt my house down, Brett." I swat over the toilet seat and relieve myself. "Who would've done something like that?" I pull my jeans backup and button them, wash my hands and leave the facility.

"Darby, I don't understand why you went back to your house." He snarls. "When I specifically…told…you to go to my house."

"Oh, so that was an order." I spat. *Something is wrong, he is trying to control me. Why?* There is momentary silence between us.

"No, I am not trying to." He sighs heavily "I want you safe… with me." Otis sees the phone to my ear as I walk toward the car.

"I want to be with you too." Otis signals me to hang up the call. "Brett, we need to leave." 'I love you."

"Darby." His voice stammers. "Darby." Disconnecting the call and shoving the phone in the back pocket of my jeans as I enter the car.

"Who was on the phone with you?" Otis stares with concern.

"Brett called me." "Why?" He starts the vehicle and then slams his other hand on the steering wheel.

"That couldn't have been Brett." "I didn't give you the new phone." Otis's redden forehead wrinkles and his eyes glare at me. "How?"

"I called him at the apartment on Rudy's phone." I feel the urge to run. "After the men attacked us."

"Darby." "Don't you see Brett is the one who is leading them after us." Otis guns the car in reverse out of the old station parking lot. "They have a phone tap on Brett's line." "Give me that phone." He says gruffly. "No more calls until we are safe." I hand it to Otis, he tears the phone apart, tosses it out the open window and we quickly drive away.

It has been hours since Otis and I last spoke on the way to this secret safehouse located in nowhere USA. In the distance was a large brown brick building, looks like an old factory. I can see at least fifteen windows and six or seven vehicles parked out front as we drive toward the structure. The gated driveway opens as we approach it, Otis takes us around the back of the huge building and we pull into an underground parking structure.

"Darby, this is my family home." "Please be respectful." He sighs. *What did he mean, respectful?* "Abby is here."

"What?" I stare at him "How?"

"I saved her from being deported." His eyes twinkle. "I married her." Otis's cheeks blush. "I love her too."

"Oh, that's nice." I say in disbelief, opening the door to get out. "Where is she?" And I shut the door, turning to follow Otis and Abby is standing by the entrance.

"Darby, you're okay." Abby walks quickly to me. "I'm glad to see you." She hugs me and whispers. *"Get out." "Go to Brett's mansion." "It's not safe."*

"Abby, how are you?" I smile. "Besides a married woman." She takes my hand, I feel a metal object in her grasp; then Abby releases my hand it is a key, I slid it into my jean pocket quickly. *"What is it for?"* I whisper to her before Otis kisses her cheek and goes inside.

"I'll tell you later." Abby speaks softly. "Now follow me."

On the inside of the bricked building, it is posh like a polished grand palace; the chandeliers are shiny and bright, the floors are glossy and slick, it is too clean to be lived in. Where are the shoes, sweaters and why isn't a television on? It is almost eerie in here, Abby takes my hand again and leads me upstairs; we enter a large room at the end of the hall and she shuts the door behind her.

"Abby, what's going on here?" She places a finger over her lips and then mouths "We can't talk here."

"This is your room, until it is safe for you to leave." Abby smiles. "Otis's family will be here shortly." "I'll come get you when they arrive." She reaches for the door handle.

"Don't leave me, Abby." I frown. "I-I don't want to be alone."

"Rest up." "I'll be back soon." Abby stares at the floor. "I am going to see Otis, now." Then she looks at me with empty eyes and leaves the room.

I walk around this huge room, studying the trinkets on each dresser and chest of drawers, admiring the four-post bed; then looking out the window as the sun begins to set, I see someone running from this building, taking a second to look behind to see if anyone follows and disappearing into the woods. Knocking at the door shakes me from my investigation, Abby enters looking amazing in her pink chiffon dress, smiling with a beautiful emerald green chiffon dress in hand.

"It is time to get dressed for dinner." She hands it to me. "I'll help you." "If you want me too."

"Yes, please." Abby hugs me, the tears form at the edges of my eyes. "I am scared, Abby." I breathe. Her arms tighten around me.

"I know you are, so am I." She whispers. I hug her back. "We will get out of here together." "Ok, let's get ready." Abby speaks in her normal tone. "The family will be waiting."

Not long after, Abby and I are walking down the long stairwell to the large dining room to meet Otis's family and friends. As we enter they introduce themselves one by one to me, I recognized one of the men from the old hotel by the cabin where Rudy and I hid for a while, it is Nicola Patrova. Why is he here? I smile shaking hands as my thoughts run wild. If he is a friend of Otis's family, then he could be the reason why this is all happening. Abby stares at me while we stroll to the table arm and arm, we sit at the table simultaneously.

"Darby, what's wrong?" Abby whispers.

"Nothing yet." I look at her, concerned. "I am figuring things out."

"Would you ladies like to take a walk after dinner?" Otis walks beside us at the table.

"Yes, I would." I sputter. "Abby, how about you?"

"Sure, Otis." She smiles.

"Great." He takes the seat next to Abby and softly touches her hand. "You look amazing Abby."

"Thank you, Otis." Abby kisses his cheek.

"Welcome new friends, I am Archibald Bosworth." Standing tall at the end of the long table. "I have the pleasure of introducing our newest family member." He says with pride. "Otis's beautiful wife, Abby." Otis stands, he takes Abby's hand and she stands next to him smiling. The family and friends clap as do I and then Otis kisses her fully on her lips. "Congratulations." Abby and Otis return to their seats as does Archibald.

Once the food is served, several conversations start throughout dinner and the volume rises. Otis, Abby and I laugh at one of his cousin's many jokes. The dinner plates are removed, we enter the ballroom where dessert is now served; then the music starts, people begin to flutter to the dance floor, it is a perfect time to escape outside.

"Otis, it is time for the walk in the garden." Abby announces. "Darby?" Otis looks at his mate, sadly.

"Yes, fresh air would be great." I reply

"Ok, ladies let's take a stroll." He takes both our arms, leading us out to the rose gardens where it is quiet, and no one follows. "Abby, I don't like this plan." His voice goes horse. "I love you."

"Otis, it will be okay." Abby smiles adoringly at her husband. "I will come back to you." "I love you, too." I knew now, it wasn't just a marriage of convenience, it is true love.

"Abby, I don't want to be the cause of you two separating." I speak up. "I can leave alone."

"No way." Abby states vibrantly. "Brett would kill me himself." She continues. "Otis, did you park the car on the other side of the woods?"

"Yes darling, I did it right before dinner." He adds.

"Wait, I saw someone leave the building right before sunset." "The person was heading into the woods."

We all stare at each other, Otis starts to pace back and forth.

"I will go check on the car." He rumbles. "I hope wasn't Nicola."

"Why don't we all go together?" I stare at them, hopeful. "That way we can all leave together."

"It could work, but Otis would have to stay behind." Abby touches his hand. "Wilhem Patrova is dangerous." Otis takes my hand and smiles.

"Darby keep my Abby safe." Otis vents, his eyes tear up. "Abby, you keep your promise." He quickly walks away.

"Darby let's go." Abby's voice shimmies. "Otis will be okay." We walk fast into the woods and stop in front of a huge old oak tree; then Abby reaches inside of a hole in the tree, pulling out a back pack with clothes in it. "Change quickly." She throws jeans and a t-shirt to me and undresses herself. "Put the dress and shoes in the back pack." Abby says breathless, then stuffs the over-stuffed pack back in the hole in the oak tree; we run bare foot through the rest of the woods until we reach the car. "Do you have the key?" I slide it out of my bra and hand it to her; she smiles, pops the trunk and hands me a pair of sneakers. "Let's get out of here." Abby starts the car and we drive away.

"Where are we going, Abby?" I ask, after my long silence. "And I want to know what is happening."

"I thought you knew." Abby gives a half laugh. "Figures Brett never told you." She snickers. "Rudy, did he say anything unusual about Brett's past?" I stare confused. "No, I guess he didn't either."

"Okay, so I've been lied too." "Again." Now, I can feel the anger well-up inside me. "Enough games, Abby." "I want the truth."

"You deserve the truth, Darby." Abby stops the vehicle. "I can only tell you the parts I know." She sighs. "But, Brett needs to come clean to you." Abby steers the car onto the open highway to somewhere that we drive for a few hours

The story begins in Austria, this is where Abby first met Brett at a corporate investment meeting and she was an undercover NSA agent posing as a massage therapist. Brett was being investigated for fraudulent investments and money laundering in foreign countries; he wasn't charged because they didn't have enough evidence against his corporation.

"Brett at this time had two specialty massage parlors set up with a major hotel chain in Europe." Abby adds. "I didn't get involved with Brett, physically yet." She breaths. "Until, the third one was being furnished." "He asked me if I wanted a job working for him." "And that he would train me...personally." I place my stiff hands on my lap, trying to listen. "I am not going into any details." She states. "But there were no feelings involved between us." I begin to relax a little. "By the time, we reached the US." "We had opened nine more." Abby smiles at me. "Your salon is number thirteen." She spats reassuringly. "Once, he met you no other woman existed."

"Are you still with the NSA?" Abby nods yes. "Does he know you are still undercover?" She frowns.

"Yes." "I told him, after the indictment fell through."

"What about Detrick and Mamie?" I inquire more.

"They were sexual acquaintances, who tried to back stab Brett and me?" "I called in a favor at NSA." Abby stares at the rearview mirror. "But it had to look real, so they arrested the four of us." She looks at me. "Is your seat belt on?"

"Yes." I mumble. "Why?"

"I think we are being followed." "Hold on." The car speeds up to sixty miles per hour, the vehicle lights follow for a few miles until it turns off the road and Abby slows us down to fifty miles per hour. "Ok they're not following us."

"So, why are we hiding out?" I ask.

"Wilhem Patrova." "He is a mafia boss from Russia." Abby supplies. "Otis's father is in dealings with him." "He thinks his money went into the Allure spa." I stare out into the darkness. "So, he thinks it is his business."

"It is Brett, Otis and my business." I grumble. "Did Otis borrow money from his father for the Hotel?"

"That's the question?" Abby face is stern. "I've asked Otis about this several times, but he won't give me a straight answer."

"I think, he doesn't really know." I shift in my seat. "Or doesn't want to know."

"Yeah, I think that's true." Abby lets out a deep sigh. "I wish he…"

"Where are we?" "It looks like…" I laugh and smile. She stops the car outside of Brett's mansion; I leap out and run for the front door. Slamming into Brett's body as we land on the floor of the foyer; we smile, laugh and kiss, he helps me to my feet and I wrap my arms around his neck. "Hi, beautiful."

"I missed you, Brett." Abby walks in behind us and smiles. "We need to have a serious talk."

"Brett, did Otis make it here yet?" His eyes glisten in her direction.

"He is upstairs." Abby runs and takes two steps at a time. "Second room on the left."

"Thank you." She says almost at the top of the stairs.

"He's a lucky guy." Brett says softly.

"No, she is the lucky girl." I snuggle in closer to him.

"Yes, but I am…"

My lips are stopped by a heated set of lips crushing mine. Brett lifts me up quickly into to his arms, he starts to carry me to his bedroom upstairs.

"Wait." He stops mid-step on the stairwell. "We need to talk."

"I know." Brett sighs. "Can we talk in the morning?"

"Yes." I put a finger on his pouting lips. "But, it needs to be about everything." He smiles.

Brett continues carrying me up the stairs, opens the first door on the right to his bedroom, then places me down across his four poster-bed mattress and undresses himself slowly in front of me; his muscular frame and protruding maleness turns my internal fever on high. Brett lies over the length of my body naked, taking my arms to lay above my head to be in control, he slowly unbuttons my jeans, lifts my hips to free the jeans downward, raises my t-shirt slowly setting fiery kisses on my skin and sliding one hand down to pull my panties away from my private place to play in my liquid core. Brett slides my panties down further to my feet and off, warm kisses linger from my feet to my inner thighs getting closer to my inner lips of my core, his tongue invades my clit with passionate caresses. I let out a loud passionate sigh, wanting more; I reach for him and he slides my arms back above my head, then hauls my hips slowly into his heated rod for a euphoric ending. We fall asleep together, his arm across my body and his face near mine; until early in the morning we awake to Otis yelling out passionately, we laugh.

"I think we can be louder." Brett whispers.

"It is my turn." I announce sensually. "Your ass is mine."

"Dirty girl." He snarls sexy. "Give it your best shot."

Then a knock at our door, take us by surprise and we sit up quickly in bed. "Who is it?" Brett asks.

"It's Armand, Sir." The butler says. "Sorry to interrupt, but." His voice varies. "You have an important visitor arriving in a few minutes."

"Who, Armand?" Brett stares at me.

"The guard said it was Wilhem Patrova, Sir." My eyes widen.

"Thank you, Armand." He stares at the door. "Wake Abby and Otis, please."

"Yes, Sir." He continues. "I'll have the rest of the staff readied, as well Sir."

"Yes, please hurry." Brett gets up quickly, taking my hands. "You need to get out of here." I look baffled. "Abby will find a safe place for you both to hide."

"I am not leaving you, again." I say sternly. "What is going on?" "Why is Patrova coming here?"

"Okay, part of Otis's family is involved with the Russian Mafia." He looks with concern. "Maybe Otis used their money to fund the Allure contract." "I asked Otis." His eyes glare. "And he stared at me confused or scared, I don't know." Brett sears. "But I will get us out of this safely."

"I've known Otis, forever." Staying cool. "He's not the type of businessman who would do this."

"I agree, but sometimes when push comes to shove." Brett rattles. "Shove wins." "So, please go with Abby." I stare at him silent. "I'll find you." I leap nakedly into his frame, wrapping my legs around his waist and kiss him strongly on the lips.

"I will." His eyes twinkle. "If, you promise."

"What, Darby?" I place my hands on his bristly cheeks.

"Marry me?" I laugh.

"Yes, I will." I smile, and we kiss; then we both get our clothes on and walk downstairs. Abby and Otis are waiting for us in the kitchen. "Not so good morning, sorry."

"Oh, I beg to differ my friend." Abby smiles sweetly at her husband. "What's the plan?"

"Abby call your boss at the NSA, let him know about Patrova." She nods. "Pack a special bag for you and Darby, then get the hell out of here." Otis is startled.

"What?" He stares at Brett. "Where is my wife going?" Otis grabs Abby's hand to halt her.

"Otis, Patrova is coming here now." Abby kisses him softly, he lets her hand loose. "I'll be okay." "And Darby will be safe too." "Grab some food, Darby." "It may be awhile before we stop again."

"Okay, Abby." Brett hands me a backpack from a cabinet under the sink. "Thank you, my love." He smiles with fearful grin. "Let's go guys." "Abby, I'll meet you outside by the car." I start looking in the pantry for dry goods and Otis walks beside me.

"Great, hurry Darby." Abby quickly leaves the kitchen. "We don't have much time."

"Take care of Abby and I'll do the same for you."

Otis tries to smile. "Brett is a good person, he loves you."

"I know." I look at him swiftly. "Go help Brett, he needs you, too." I rush out of the pantry to find Abby waiting for me at the car and I get in the vehicle quickly. "Let's go." Abby steps on the gas, we leave Brett's property out the back gate. In the distance I can see four rather large vehicles driving towards Brett's mansion. "Oh no, I hope they'll be okay." She looks through the rearview mirror and takes a deep breath.

Abby and I speed off in the vehicle quickly, we are about a mile away when we hear a loud explosion; she stomps on the brakes throwing us forward to a screeching halt and we both stare out the back window looking towards Brett's mansion where there is huge plume of smoke and debris flying out from the area. We look at each other with tears of fear in our eyes, simultaneously wiping our tears away and she turns back to face the open road ahead; Abby steps on the gas and we don't speak for most of the drive to someplace west of what was Brett's mansion. Eventually, we reach a set of blinking lights that causes her to slow down the car.

"Darby." Abby's voice shutters. "This is the first time in a long time I've been afraid." She looks at me seriously. Wilhelm is very dangerous." "We need to be super careful."

"Let's keep going." I face the reflection in the window. "I am scared too." "I hope they…"

"Let's…not think about it." Abby cuts me off. "We are going to my grandfather's house?" Her lips snicker. "It is abandoned." "He left it to me, before I was born." She continues driving. "It has been kept up by my cousin Theo." "It is still a few hours away."

I lay my head back against the seat and rest. "We can stop in few miles to take a break, if you want?"

"Yes, that would be great." I agree. "I need to stretch my legs." *Brett, I hope I see you again. I whisper to myself.*

"Me, too." We laugh a little, all the while wanting to cry over not knowing if they are alive or dead.

After an hour or two, we stop a few miles out from Abby's grandfather's place to stretch and grab some groceries at a little market with a gas station right next door. The way Abby moves about you can tell she is familiar with her surroundings, I follow her with some certainty that we will be alright; until we reach the counter to pay, she stares at the mid-aged man behind the register who smiles at her, quickly taking the items and bagging them in paper bags.

"Well, Abby are you going to speak?" The clerk says, and she continues to stare at him.

"Hi, my name is Darby." Trying to change the silence between them. "And you are?"

"The-o." Abby slurs out.

"What?" I stare at them.

"I am Theo." He grimaces. "Abby's cousin."

"It nice to meet you Theo." I reply kindly. "Abby, snap out of it." I shake her arm.

"I am so sorry Theo." Abby blurbs. "I didn't recognize you at first." She smiles. "You've grown up so much since the last time I saw you."

"Yes cousin, in ten years." His eyes sparkle. "Things change as do people." We all laugh together.

"Can I have the key to Grandfather's house?" Abby asks politely. "We came to stay for a while."

"Sure." Theo says, fishing in his jeans pockets. "I get out of here in ten minutes." He hands Abby the key. "I can meet you there."

"How much do we owe you?" I add, taking out a wad of bills from my pocket.

"Nothing," Theo answers as I stuff the money back in my pocket. "I have a tab here." Abby and I grab the bags, I wave bye to him on the way out the door.

"I need to get gas next door." Abby says opening the trunk stuff with two pre-packed suitcases, shoving the bags to make room for the groceries.

"Why were you staring at him?" I ask handing her the next bag. "He seems very nice."

"He looks like his father." Abby speaks softly, stuffing the last bag in the truck. "His father wasn't so nice to me." She slams the truck lid down.

"Oh, okay." I can tell she doesn't want talk about what happened.

"Get in." We both enter the car, she drives us next door to pump gas and we leave the station to go to her grandfather's old house.

The next twenty minutes goes by fast when we pull into a long driveway that take us to a small grey two-story southern style mansion with patios that run the length of the top and bottom floors, it is amazing. The gravel road into the circle drive crunches under the tires as we pull in to stop, I open the door and step out smiling, Abby gets out too.

"Why wouldn't want to live here?" I gasp. "It is gorgeous, amazing even."

"Some of my memories are really wonderful." Abby sighs. "But the others are dark and unforgiving."

"What?" She walks to the front door, leaving me to stare at her. Seconds later, I shut the door to the car and follow her inside. "Abby, are you alright?"

"I'll be fine." She mumbles back. "Just me and an old ghost."

"An old ghost?" I ask with curiosity. "You're Grandfather?"

"No, I didn't know him." Abby teeters a little. "My Uncle, Theo's dad." She slumps down in a chair by the open door. "I used to love coming out here in the summer with my parents and brothers." Abby's mind reflects. "Theo's Dad used to be the caretaker." She smiles. "Until he died twelve years-ago." Her eyes turn to mine. "He hurt…raped me when I was fourteen." I gasp aloud. "My own father didn't believe me." She continues, and her hands shake with each word. "But Theo…saw what happened." "And."

"And I saved you from your father's wrath." Theo says as he enters the dwelling. "Your mother showed up here a few hours later with your brothers." He tugs Abby up from her seat and hugs her tightly.

"Yes, she slapped my father for not believing me." Abby spouts pushing him away. "And we left here to go back to the city, never to spend another summer here again."

"I love you, Abby." Theo speaks sincere. "My father can't hurt you anymore." His face softens. "The sooner you let the bad memories go, the better."

"I have…being here made them all swell-up." She is teary-eyed but smiles again. "Let's bring in the groceries and suitcases."

We all go outside to the car and once everything is inside and put away; we relax on the top floor patio overlooking Lake Pinelock with a cool beverage in hand. Theo tells me a story of when Abby and he learned how to swim in this lake. His father made him climb up the tire swing and drop into the water, but Abby wouldn't do it, she was afraid to drown.

> "So, my father found an old black inner tube, filled with air; he told her to float out to the middle of the lake and swim back. Abby liked the idea of the inner tub and floating, but my father didn't tell her that it had a leak in it and she would sink." I stare at Theo.
>
> "Why would he do something like that to his niece?" I ask appalled.
>
> "He didn't care, I guess." Theo states.
>
> "No, my Uncle didn't believe in fear." "He used to say fear can kill you if you're not careful." Abby supplies. "I guess he figure if I didn't try to swim I would drown."
>
> "What happened?" I look at Abby.
>
> "My mother showed up in a nick of time." Abby smiles. "She swam out to me and carried me into shore on her back." Her mouth shimmies. "My mom told my Uncle that she would teach me how to swim without his help."
>
> "Your Mom didn't like your Uncle, did she?" I inquire.
>
> "Not at all." Abby laughs. "She told me once that she begged her father not to let my Uncle be the caretaker of this property if something happened to him." She rubs her eyes and continues. "That my father and she could take care of the place." "Unfortunately, he disagreed because it was too much to handle, there was five of us and it was only My Uncle and Theo."
>
> "Okay, but how did you inherit this place?" I lookout towards the lake with a smile. "Why you?"

"The short answer is because I wasn't born yet when he died to form an opinion of him." Abby stands walks to the railing. "Was he a bastard, no." "So, I gathered." Abby breaths in deep. "But because my mother married twice she no longer could inherit his estate." "And my Uncle's father was the original caretake, the job was passed down from generation to generation."

"Now, it my job until Abby says goodbye to Theo." He jaunts. We all laugh.

"Theo, I got married two months ago, but I don't know if my husband is still alive." Theo glazes in disbelief at Abby. "We were in danger before we arrived, I had to leave without him."

"What?" He looks upset. "Are you still working with NSA or for Brett Slade?"

"Both, I guess." Abby yawns. "I have to call the field office tomorrow at six a.m. sharp." I breath out a sigh, the colors are beautifully shimmering over the water of Lake Pinelock at sunset.

"Anyone hungry?" Theo announces. "I can cook dinner for the weary travelers."

"Yes, I could eat some food." I smile at him. "Abby are you hungry?" We look over at Abby, she has fallen asleep in the chair. "I guess, not." Theo smiles and picks her up from the chair. "I'll hold the door open for you." He smiles.

"I am going to take her to her room." Theo speaks quietly. "Meet you in the kitchen." I nod yes with weary smile.

I take the drink glasses with me inside, walking slowly down the narrow dark stairwell to the modern styled kitchen. I open the stainless-steel doors to the fridge, grabbing the bottle of previously opened wine and pouring more of its sweet indulgence in my glass. The doors swing shut, Theo walks into the kitchen at the same time, he touches my glass and smiles.

"I think you should eat before you drink more." His eye glimmer with a Cheshire cat grin. "I don't think I could carry you to bed too." He touches his back.

"I am a big girl, but food is a good idea." I smile back. "Can I help?"

"No, it is okay." Theo pulls out a pot and frying pan with familiarity. "I enjoy cooking, I find it relaxing."

"I promise I will drink this glass of wine slowly." He laughs. "If I-I…" Theo turns on a radio next to the stove playing up beat dance music. "I guess I won't fall asleep waiting." His body starts swaying to the music while cooking at the stove, then sings the words to the song and dances a swing step to the fridge to grab other items out. *Theo is full entertainment. I thought.* My cellphone rings in my pocket, pulling it out I stare at the number, it is Brett's; should I answer it or not?

"Are you going to get it?" Theo sees the fear in my eyes, walking over to me and takes the phone out of my hand. "I'll answer it." He smiles at me. "Hello, who is this?" He returns to the stove to stir the ingredients in the pot "No." "There is no one here by that name, sorry." Theo gives me back the cellphone. "The man asked for Otis Boswell." "Who is he?"

"Abby's husband." Sad, I look down at the floor. "He was my friend, too."

"What happened before you got here?" Theo asks.

"An explosion of everything." I utter with tears of sadness. "The Archibald and Wilhelm connection, I guess." I cry out. "That's all I know…." "And I don't know if Brett's alive or dead." I feel the emptiness seeping inside.

"Okay, I think I can help you and Abby." Theo suggests. "I have a friend who lives in Big Bay, she works at the hospital." He touches my hand, continues. "I could call her to ask about the casualties of the explosion." I smile.

"I don't want to get you involved." I take the Kleenex he offers and wipe my tears. "Abby would get upset."

"My friend will be discreet." Theo sparks. "I think Abby would happy to know if her husband is alive or not." I nod with a smile.

"We will eat dinner and I will call her later." I help with the plates and utensils, he fills the dishes with a delicious concoction.

"This food tastes wonderful, Theo." I take another bite. "You should be a Chef."

"I was at a big restaurant in New York City before my father died." I stare at him curiously. "Why did I give up a prestigious job to be a caretaker?"

"Yes, why would you?" I grimace at him.

"I made a promise to my grandfather, that if my father died, I would take-over as caretaker until Abby was ready to live here."

"Honorable." I take bite of food, stopping for a moment. "But crazy." He laughs, finishing his plate of food and drink a bottle of imported beer.

"Are you done?" His dirty plate in hand. "I can take if it…" I stand and take the plate out of his hand, placing it on top of mine.

"I'll do the dishes, you made dinner." He smiles brightly taking out his cellphone.

"Great." "I will call Daphne." He walks outside the kitchen to the patio. I fill the sink with hot water and soap, placing the dirty dishes inside the watery sink; when I finish washing and drying everything, Theo walks inside the kitchen solemnly. "It's not good news, but it isn't totally bad."

"Tell me, Theo." I ask returning to my seat at the table. "What is it?"

"There was eight people pulled out of the mansion." He sits across from me, touches my hand softly. "The five dead were identified as Brett's house staff, two were sent to another hospital for severe burns and the last one is on life support at her hospital, they are comparing dental records on him."

"Okay, the survivors could be Brett and Otis, right?" I try to be positive but feel unsteady.

"Daphne said she would call her friend at the other hospital to find out the condition of the other people."

"So, we wait." I sigh. "Well, I am going to bed." "Theo, show me the way to my room." Theo takes my hand and leads the way upstairs to a room on the left.

"Abby is next door." He opens the door. "I am down there." Pointing to the other side of the hallway. "First door on the right." He walks away.

"Goodnight, Theo." I smile. "Thank you for dinner."

"Your welcome." He waves. "Thank you for being here for Abby."

The room has soft lighting and big soft four post bed, I climb under the covers fully clothed and fall asleep instantly. Sometime in the darkness, hear creaking floor boards, voices speaking gruffly, and a door slamming shut; I sit up startled, my heart pounding hard in my chest, I look around it is morning as the sun peeks through my bedroom window. "Wow, what dream." I say aloud. I get up, go to the bathroom to wash my face, brush my teeth and change into clean clothes from the suitcase sitting on the dresser. I wonder if Abby's already up, I leave my room and stop to knock on her door.

"Abby, it's Darby." I say loudly. "Hey Abby."

"She is downstairs, Darby." Theo answers from the stairwell. "In the kitchen."

"Hey, did Daphne call you back?" He smiles walking towards me.

"Yes, still not sure of the identity of the man in the burn unit." "But they confirmed that man at hospital in Big Bay is Otis." I smile big.

"Abby must be happy." I smile slightly.

"Yeah, she wants to go see him." My eyes get very big.

"No, no she can't do that." I walk quickly down the stairs. "Wilhelm will kill her."

"What?" Theo says forceful. "He'll what?" He follows right behind me to the kitchen.

"Abby, you can't go to Otis?" She stares at me with a serious look. "Wilhelm will kill you." Abby shuts her eyes and her body shakes, I go to her, hugging her body tightly. "I know you love him, but he wouldn't want you to risk it." She cries harder. "I don't know if one of the men in the burn unit, is Brett."

"Okay, I won't go." Abby says between sobs. "He knows me." "Otis will find me when he is able."

"Brett has no family, but us." She looks at me. "How are they going to identify him?" I give her a Kleenex, she smiles. "Does he have any dental records?" I cry.

"If Brett is alive, he will find you." Abby stands up in front of me. "You are the love of his life." We hug again and smile.

Later that afternoon, Abby and Theo have the long-awaited talk; she releases him from his caretaker duties, assumes control of her mansion and the monies left for her. Theo writes down Daphne's phone number for Abby before he leaves us a few days later; he decides to return to New York City to find a Chef's position at a fine restaurant. A few more weeks go by, Abby still hasn't heard from Daphne. It is Abby's turn to make lunch and my turn to set the table; she starts cooking food on the stove, stops to grab her cellphone and I sit at the set table, watching her pace a little and wonder who she called.

"Daphne, it is Abby." The nurse sounds happy. "How is he doing?" She is listening to Daphne. "That's great." Abby smiles. "He did." She stirs the ingredients in the pot. "Thanks, bye."

"What happened?" I look at her curiously. "Is he okay?"

"Yes, Daphne said he was walking yesterday." Abby takes deep breath. "He's asking for me." I smile. "Daphne told him when he gets well." The tears of joy escape her eyes. "He'll know where to find me." I jump up from my seat to hug her.

"I am so happy for you." I state. "Anything on the other men in the other hospital."

"She is calling today for an update." She smiles. "I hope for your sake it is Brett." I grimace unconvincingly.

"Oh-h, I only wish I knew if he was alive or not." I squirm a little. "It is …impossible."

"I understand, Darby." Abby touches my shoulder. "If I didn't know about Otis, I'd be in your boat."

"Thanks, Abby." She walks over to the stove. I return to my seat at the table, I still feel an emptiness inside as I stare out the window next to me. *I miss you, Brett.*

"Lunch is ready." Abby looks at me, I am still staring out the window. "Hey." "Darby, are you okay?" she says it a little louder. "Darby." I jump a little.

"Oh shit." I turn my head to look at her wiping tears from my eyes. "Yeah, I'm okay." Abby carries two plates of food over to the table, placing one in front of me.

"No, you're not okay." She sits across from me. "I am so sorry, that I."

"No, please don't be sorry." I try to smile, touching her hand across the table. "I am really happy for you and Otis."

"Brett is very lucky to have you." Abby smiles, says sincerely. "And I truly hope he makes it home to you."

The rest of the day goes by, as does the following weeks and few months; soon it is summertime, Otis is released from his six-month stay the hospital; he joins us at Abby's mansion, watching them be happy hasn't been easy as hold on to the hope Brett is alive and well.

It has been almost eight months since the explosion; Otis, Abby and I decide that we should take a trip to Big Bay Lake to check on the hotel and spa. Also, Abby and I never heard from Daphne about the other man's condition, Wilhelm Patrova looking for us or the authorities either; I am scared, but it has been too quiet.

"Okay, ladies." Otis proudly announces getting into the car. "Let's get going."

"Abby, I am a little nervous." I get into the back seat of the car. "How do you feel?" Abby gets in the passenger side front seat.

"I'm a little worried." She smiles back at me. "But I think we are safe."

"Ladies, I called the local police department." Otis utters putting on his seat belt. "The Captain told me that the investigation has been concluded at the Slade mansion." He sighs. "The investigators found bomb fragments in the mechanical room."

"Bomb fragments." Abby stares back at me. "What kind of bomb was it?"

"Incendiary." Otis replies. "I guess the person or persons thought the parts would burn up."

"Did they find any finger prints?" I inquire. "On the fragments." "Or anywhere else?"

"Yes, a few." He coughs. "Wilhelm's sons, Mikela." I glare at the rearview mirror. "And Nicola."

"Huh, why send his sons to do his dirty work?" I say staring out the window. "Did the police do a background checks on his sons?"

"I didn't ask." "I think or hope they would have." He smiles at Abby. "We can ask him when we get there." Otis adds. "He asks that we see him first before we go looking around town."

"Oh, we need to check-in first." I laugh still looking out the window, I get a pain in my chest as we get closer to Big Bay. "Hey Otis, can we stop at the Parkland Hospital?"

"Yeah, sure." Otis gives a sad look at Abby.

"I hope the other men they found are okay?" I breath. "Daphne never call us back."

"Darby it has been a while." Abby states. "He may not be there anymore."

"I know." I look up at the sky from the window. "But I don't want to lose hope."

Ten minutes later, we reach Parkland Hospital parking lot; Abby and I walk inside the hospital entrance while Otis parks the car. The security guard asks us who we are visiting; Abby and I explain about the explosion eight months ago and the men who were brought here for treatment. The guard calls the hospital administration in the next room and he returns a few minutes later.

"Ms. Deel, the administrator will be with you in a few minutes." The security guard says. "Please wait in the lobby." Not long after, an older gentleman walks over to where we are sitting.

"Hello, Miss Deel." His right hand reaches out. "Miss Steed and Mr. Bosworth." We all stand up. "I am the hospital Administrator, Arthur Donovan." "How can I help you?" Otis, Abby and I take turns shaking his hand.

"Mr. Donovan, I am inquiring about the men who was brought here after the explosion at the Slade mansion." I breath in deeply. "Did you identify them?"

"Yes, it took a while." Mr. Donovan smile. "One was badly burned." He places his left hand in his pants pocket. "Unfortunately, the second man we are unable to release his identity."

"Why?" I stare at him curiously.

"Per the patient's request." Mr. Donovan replies shifting his weight to his right side. "Besides, he is no longer here." "We released him one month ago."

"Do you have a forwarding address or phone number?" I gasp, the tears stream down my cheeks. "I need to find out if he is Brett Slade." My voice shrills. "I-I."

"I'm sorry Ms. Deel." Mr. Donovan takes out a hanky from his suit pocket. "I am not allowed to release that information either." I dab my wet cheeks with the hanky Mr. Donovan hands me and plop back into the chair behind me. "But if you get a court order I would be happy to help you."

"Thank you for your help, Mr. Donovan." Abby declares holding Otis's hand in hers. "We understand." The administrator walks away. "Darby let's go to the police station." She touches my hand and smiles. "Maybe they can get us the court order."

"I know a Judge in the court house." Otis pipes up. "She owes me a favor." Abby and I look at him.

"Well, let's go to the courthouse." I try to be happy. "Otis." We all walk outside to the parked car and drive toward the courthouse in town.

"Otis, honey aren't we supposed to stop at the police station first."

"Yes, darling." Otis smiles at his wife. "It is next door to the courthouse."

After parking in the visitor parking lot; we enter the police station and ask for the Captain. The desk Sargent directs towards the Captain's office; he is standing in the hallway next to the door to his office waiting for us. The Captain is a short stout balding structure, he waves us inside his office.

"Please take a seat." As he shows us into his office. "How may I help you?" He sits in his chair behind the rather large desk.

"Hi, Captain James." Otis speaks up. "I called yesterday and spoke to you." He continues. "My name is Otis Bosworth."

"Yes, I remember." His face lightens. "And this is Ms. Deel and Ms. Steed, correct."

"Yes Sir." I add. "If I may."

"Sure, go ahead young lady." Captain James stares at me. "How can I help you?"

"I would like to ask for a court order." I spill out. "My fiancé is Brett Slade." I lean forward. "He may be the one of the men who had been burned in the explosion at the Slade mansion." I take a deep breath and the Captain nods. "But the hospital won't disclose the burned man's identity without an order from the judge." A long sigh escapes me. "Can you help me?"

"Well, I will have to talk to Judge Parks." The Captain looks concern. "But if the man doesn't want he identity released." "There isn't much I can do." His voice stutters. "You understand."

"Yes." I feel a let-down coming, but I try to ignore it. "I do."

"Captain James, not to worry." Otis chimes in. "Judge Parks is a friend." "I can talk to her on Darby's behalf."

"Son sounds good, she and I don't always see eye to eye." The Captain stands up. "If you need anything else." "Please do stop by the station."

"Thank you, Captain James." Abby says, then we all get up, leave his office and the police station.

We walk next door to the courthouse; Otis requests to see Judge Parks today, her schedule will be open in an hour and his appointment is made. Meanwhile, Otis takes us to the Big Bay Hotel and the spa; both places are looking great and running smoothly. Abby's friend Paige has been running 'Allure Me' with Jimmy and Alexandra, who are doing the massages for the special clients; Sasha has been managing the hotel in Otis's absence, too.

An hour later, we return to the courthouse and wait while Otis speaks to Judge Parks, she agrees to give us the order. On the way back to Parkland Hospital, we stop by the empty lot where my house stood, then vacant land where Brett's mansion used to be too. I decide to get out of the car, standing near the circle driveway in front of where Brett's place stood, looking down at the ground I get the feeling someone watching me. I look up quickly from the ground toward the woods on the left of the property, there is a man standing in the distance staring at me; I can't tell who it is, so I start running toward him, he turns quickly and disappears into the woods. Once I reach the edge of the woods, I call out to him again and again; he doesn't reply but, I can feel that he is near by watching me. Not long after, Abby and Otis appear behind me.

"Darby, who was that?" Abby says half-out of breath. "Do you think it could be Brett?"

"I don't know." I keep staring into the woods. "The man was too far away." My heart is beating fast. "I-I hope so." Otis walks past me, as Abby and I stand still, waiting for the man to appear.

"Otis, find him if you can." Abby hollers out to him.

"I'll do my best, darling." He yells back running off into the heavily wooded area.

"Be careful." She says staring out to where Otis disappears into the woods and then to me. "Let's walk towards the back gate."

"Yeah, maybe he went that way." My heart leaps.

We quickly walk around the thickest part of the woods to the back gate; the whole time I feel like his eyes are watching me all the way there. Once we reach the gate there is a man standing there in a dark blue hoodie with the hood covering his face; his body sways back and forth, as if he is ready to run away.

"Who are you?" I yell. "What are you doing here?" The man standing still, not saying anything. "Why won't you answer me?" I walk slowly towards him and stop; he is anxious and starts to sway again. "Brett is it you." My voice calmly utters, the man's head tilts up a little; then he turns and runs away from us. "Stop, don't leave!" Otis's form peaks out of the woods and runs after the hooded man but, stops once he runs through the gate.

"Otis are you, all right?" Abby says breathless once we reach the gate opening.

"Yes." He puffs out of breath.

"Did you see his face?" I blurt out. "Who is it?"

"The man has a scarred face from burns." He eyes open wide. "I didn't recognize him." "He ran off too fast." Sadly, I look down at the ground wanting to cry.

"Darby, it could be Brett." Otis touches my shoulder. "Maybe." I look up at them both and smile.

"Yeah, Darby." Abby smiles. "Don't lose hope."

"I won't." My heart aches when I speak. "I just miss him." "Otis." I feel a spark of enlightenment. "Abby." "We need to find Daphne."

"Why?" Abby sputters. "Oh, you think she never asked." Her eyes widen. "About the other man."

Abby understands that Daphne may have known all along who the unknown man was and lied for him. "Otis, get the car." She rattles out. "We need to go to Big Bay Hospital pronto."

"Yes, darling." He runs off toward the direction of the parked car.

"Darby, she lied to us." I nod.

"I know." Still looking at the open gate. "I never felt comfortable with Daphne's help."

Otis pulls up next to us in the car a few minutes later and we drive to Big Bay Hospital. In ten minutes, we reach the hospital parking lot and Otis's cellphone rings.

"Hello, this Otis Bosworth." The voice speaks over the phone. "Yes, Captain James." Otis is listening to the man speaking. "Yes, good news." "Okay see you soon." He turns his phone off and smiles. "The judge delivered the court order." "Captain James is meeting us here in a few minutes." We sit in the car until Captain James arrives.

"Hello." "Otis, Abby and Darby." Captain James smiles, as we get out of the car. "Here is the court order releasing information from this hospital and Parkland too."

"That's great." I reply. "Thank you."

"Oh, no worries." The Captain laughs. "Let's go investigate."

Inside the hospital Captain James shows his badge at the front desk and asks to see the administrator, while we wait in the lobby area.

The administrator is a tall grey-haired woman in her sixties, dressed in charcoal business suit; she walks with Captain James over to us in the lobby.

"This is Greta Lang she is the hospital's administrator." Captain James states. "I explain the situation to her and she has agreed to help us."

"Hi, Ms. Lang." I smile at her. "My name is Darby Deel."

"Yes, I know who you are." Ms. Lang reaches out her boney fingers to grasp my hand. "Your Mom and I were good friends."

"Oh, you knew my Mom." I smile more at ease. "Can you tell me anything about the burned man from the accident at the Slade estate?"

"Well, I know they couldn't identify him at first." She sighs. "But when he woke up at Parkland Hospital his identity was hushed."

"Why?" I stare at her curiously.

"He is a contributor to the hospital financially." Ms. Lang says as matter of fact. My thoughts race, Brett is a businessman and he makes lots of money. "The man asked for non-disclosure of his identity."

"Well, it is time to expose his identity." I brightly announce. "We have a court order."

"Yes, Ma'am." Captain James smiles. "But we need to go to Parkland Hospital." "Thank you, Ms. Lang for you time." He looks at her directly. "Please do not speak of this meeting to anyone."

"Yes, Sir." Ms. Lang looks at little startled. "I will not." The three of us see something strange when their conversation ended but dismiss it.

We leave Big Bay hospital; Captain James police car is in the lead and we follow behind him to Parkland Hospital. The security guard direct us to Mr. Donovan's office and he greets us as we enter; Captain James hands him the court order, he reads it and his smile goes to a frown quickly.

"I will release this information, but it can only be given to Ms. Deel." Otis and Abby look at him strange at first.

"We will wait for you in the lobby." Otis takes his wife's hand, they leave Mr. Donovan's office.

"Captain James, only Ms. Deel please." Mr. Donovan asks. Captain James mumbles and leaves the office too. "Ms. Deel, would you mind closing the door?" I comply.

"Okay." I sit in the chair next to his desk. "Please tell me who he is?"

"I will, but there is something I must say first." I stare at him.

"Go on." I utter.

"Mr. Bosworth was sent to Big Bay and the other two victims were sent here to our burn unit." He swallows roughly, and I continue to stare at him. "The first man was burned very badly." "The second one, not burned as bad." Mr. Donovan smirks. "We identified the first burn victim, it was Wilhelm Patrova's son Mikela and he died shortly after arriving here." "The second man asked not to be identified, his face was burnt and needed a lot of reconstructive surgery." I held my breath though his lengthy explanation. "Once the burns healed, he left our hospital to go abroad for further surgeries."

"Okay, tell me who he is?" I plead. "I want know, now."

"It was…Nicola Patrova." Mr. Donovan sighs. "Wilhelm Patrova's other son."

"What?" "Where is Brett?" I am stunned, feeling let down. "He has to be alive."

"Mr. Slade wasn't pulled out of the rumble." Mr. Donovan declares. "Maybe he is hiding…or not."

"Or not?" I cry. "I need to find him." I stand, run out of his office through the lobby and outside. Otis and Abby give chase after I run past them in the lobby.

"Darby, stop!" Abby hollers. "Please." Otis and Abby stand next to me as I stop next to the car breathing heavy. "What happened in there?"

"We need to retrace our steps." I bellow. "Starting with the cabin and the old hotel."

"What about Patrova, he'll still might be after you?" Otis pipes in. "He thinks you'll lead him to Brett."

"Well, that's the chance we need to take." I argue. "If Brett's in hiding, we need to find him first."

"Darby, are you sure?" Abby inquires. "You may be getting in too deep."

"Abby, I love Brett." I say teary-eyed. "I need to know if he is… okay." She smiles.

"Okay, where is the cabin?" Otis asks.

"It is at Big Buck Lake." He nods. "About two hours away."

Meanwhile, Captain James is watching us from his police vehicle; we get into Otis's car to drive to Big Buck Lake and he follows us, staying out of sight. A few hours later, I know we are getting closer to the cabin, the bumps in the road give it away.

"Otis we are about two miles away from the cabin." I smile. "If you take the next left, we can go to the old hotel first." He looks in the rearview mirror at me and smiles. "I hope…he is there." I gasp.

As we approach the old hotel, we notice three large trucks and a group of at least fifty workers; so, Otis parks the car in the woods off the road and we get out to investigate. It appears they are demolishing the old hotel; the workers are using heavy equipment to break the concrete floors and walls, and trucks are hauling it away. I recognize an older man in a yellow hard hat, it is Wilhelm Patrova. I tap Abby on the shoulder and point to him, she glares at him. Otis motions over to the other side of the hotel, it is Captain James; he is walking over to Patrova, smiles and shakes his hand. Otis looks at us and points back to the car; we all walk back to the vehicle.

"What is Captain James doing with Patrova?" Otis spats out. "Is he in it with him?"

"I don't know." Abby adds. "But I don't like it."

"I am not sure what we saw." I add. "But I let's get to the cabin it is getting dark outside."

We drive a quarter of mile down the dirt road and pull into a skinny drive way to the cabin. From the roadway, it looks like there is a fire going inside the cabin, someone is there. I hurry out of the car, opening the door to the cabin and Brett is standing in front of me, scarred and torn; I wrap my arms around his neck and hold him close as the tears flow down my cheeks.

"Darby." Brett cries. "I-I." He tries to push me away.

"I am so happy your alive." I kiss his damaged lips and hold him closer. "I love you so much."

"Don't…love me." Brett panics and shoves me away harder. "I am hideous." I push his hands away.

"What?" I place his matted face in my hands. "No."

"It is only the outside of you that's a mess." "I love the inside, where your heart is mine."

"Stop it, Darby." Brett barks. "I can't do this." He walks toward the fireplace, I stomp in after him.

"Yes, you can." I declare unmoving, standing right beside him. "I haven't spent the last eight months in hiding and waiting for you." He grabs the half empty whiskey bottle of the table. "For you to give up on us now." Otis and Abby are standing in the doorway.

"Well, hello Otis and Abby." Brett surges, taking a drink from the whiskey bottle; they walk inside and shut the door behind them. "You are looking well, Otis."

"Brett." Abby speaks.

"Abby." Brett sarcastically mimics her.

"I see, you and whiskey." Abby grumbles. "Not a good combination." She takes the bottle out of his hand. "Otis, I think he needs a nap." Otis directs Brett to the bedroom.

"Brett, what the hell are you doing?" Otis stares at him next to the bed. "I know you hurting, but don't take out on the one who loves you." He helps Brett on the bed. "She never gave up on you."

"I-I know." Brett mumbles off to sleep and Otis returns to the living room. "But, I am a mess."

"Darby and I are going to see what's in the kitchen." Abby smiles at him. "I love you, Otis."

In the kitchen, the refrigerator is fully stocked with food and the pantry as well. Abby and I decide to make dinner, the smell from the kitchen bellows into the living room waking Otis from his catnap and Brett from is drunken nap. They both waltz into the kitchen, Brett pulls the dark blue hoodie over his face; I walk over to him confidently, slowly pull it back uncovering his face, I smile letting him know it is okay. We all sit together at the table to eat dinner.

"This dinner is wonderful." Otis says with his mouthful. "Ladies, you did good." We smile.

"Oh-h, I can taste it." Brett excitedly speaks after his long silence. "I haven't been able to taste anything since…the explosion." His eyes sparkle. "It is delicious."

"Brett, how long have you been here?" I ask.

"I came here after I left Parkland." Nervous, he shifts his weight to left in the chair. "I wanted to see you, all of you." I look at him and touch his hand resting on the table. "But I remember you saying something about the old hotel."

"They are demolishing it." Otis interjects. "And Wilhelm Patrova is overseeing it." Brett sits up straight.

"What?" His body begins to shake uncontrollably.

"Relax, Brett." I cry out, getting up from my chair quickly and trying to hold him still. "Please relax

"I can't control it." Brett's voice shakes. "My pills are in the bedroom on the nightstand." Abby runs out of the kitchen to get them; Otis hears noise from outside and looks out the window.

"I will hold you until it stops." I whisper in his ear and I can feel the tremors slowing down. "I love you, Brett."

"I know." He tries to whisper back. "I love you, too."

"Here you go." Abby says out of breath, noticing his shaking has stopped. "Oh, you're okay."

"Thanks, Abby." I look at her with a smile. "He's going to be fine."

"I see that." Abby looks over at Otis. "What's wrong, Otis?"

"I think we need to leave here, soon." Otis utter aloud. "Patrova has more men arriving." He stares out the window. "It won't be long until he finds us."

"I am tired of running, Otis." Brett states strongly. "What is it, Otis?" Otis looks at Brett's scars. "What aren't you telling us?"

"I-I made a big mistake." We all stare at Otis.

"What is it?" Abby glares at him. "What did you do?"

"I-I may have used Patrova's money." Otis says quietly.

"What?!" Brett is very upset.

"I thought my father." Otis breaths out. "Stopped working with Patrova years ago." He stalls. "But, the Allure inadvertently could be his." I fall back against the wall, staring at Brett and Otis. "I am sorry, Darby." I start crying, everything that has happened in last year finally breaks me part.

"Darby, we don't know if it is true." Abby tries to console me, the tears stream down my cheeks. "Right, Brett."

"Yes, Abby." Brett answer not convincingly. "Otis and I will fix this." He tries to take my hand, but I push away from the wall; walk into the living room and sit on the sofa in front of the fireplace. "Darby."

Brett slides in next to me on the sofa, I feel his breath on my neck, sending tingles down my spine. "I didn't know, I promise." I look at him, pulling him close.

"I believe you." I kiss him softly on the lips, he is stiff. "Kiss me." I whisper, he doesn't move. "Kiss me." I say it a little louder, he still doesn't move. "Kiss me!" I raise my voice louder, he launches into me with a deep passionate kiss that shakes me from the inside.

"Oh, Darby." I can feel the pain releasing from inside him. "I missed you." "I wanted to run into your arms when I saw you earlier, but I was scared."

"Why?" I touch his face. "Because of the scars, we all have them." I kiss him again. "Some are on the outside and some are on the inside." He pulls me against his chest and holds me there for a moment.

"You are amazing." Brett says. "I love you."

"I know you." I laugh as Abby and Otis walk into the living room. "Hey guys." They look at us funny. "What's wrong?"

"Put out the fire, we need to go now." Abby says sternly. "They are coming."

"Wilhelm's men." Otis stutters nervously. "They were yelling my name across the lake." He looks at Brett. "And yours."

"I'll pack quickly, meet me outside." Abby comes back from the kitchen with a pail of water. "Not water, Abby." Brett stops her. "Sand." "There is a bag outside the back door." Abby drops the pail on the table in the kitchen and grabs the bag, while I help Brett pack his bag in the bedroom. "Darby, the top drawer has clothes in it." As I grab the clothes, there is a ring box and my heart races; I hand him the clothes and ring box. "Later." He looks at me and smiles.

"Brett, the fire is out, and the power is off." Abby rattles out. "Otis finished putting the cooler of food in the car." She leaves the doorway. "Let's go."

"Brett, are you ready to go?" I smile at him and he nods. "Let's get out of here."

"No, I want to see Wilhelm first." I stare at him. "Otis and I need to talk to him." "I am tired of running." We walk outside to the car. "Abby." Brett announces. "Stay with Darby." "Otis and I need to take care of some business."

"What?" Otis tries to drive away, when Abby pulls the key out of the ignition. "Abby, why?"

"He is right, no more hiding." Abby tells him. "What kind of life is our baby going to have if you're not here." Otis stares at her, then smiles.

"Baby?" Otis face softens. "We are having a baby." He hugs his wife. "I love you." She smiles brightly.

They leave us at the cabin alone for what seems like hours; Abby and I entertain ourselves with a few games of cards, seven card stud and poker.

"How far along are you?" I say while Abby is touching her tummy. "If."

"No, it's fine." She smiles at me. "I think almost eight weeks." "I go to the Doctor's next week." We hear a car door shut outside and they walk inside the cabin.

"What happened?" Abby stands up from the sofa. "Are we safe?" Otis hugs her. Brett sits next to me.

"Yes, for now." Otis speaks first. "Wilhelm's not taking our business away, it is not his."

"His fight is with Otis's father." Brett continues. "The explosion was an accident, Nicola wasn't supposed to blow up my house or himself."

"Mikela, gave the orders." Otis adds. "But the bomb was for my parents' mansion, not Brett's.

"Wilhelm offered to pay for my cosmetic surgery." Brett states. "I declined." He looks at me. "But I agreed on him rebuilding our home." My spirits lift, and I feel relief.

"Our home, sound nice." I snuggle against his chest.

"We can all go back to civilization again." Otis says happily. "The room and room service at the Big Bay Hotel are on us." He pulls Abby close. "Let's go home." She smiles.

In a few more hours, Brett and I comfortable in our hotel room waiting for room service to bring us a late-night snack, the knock on the door indicates it is here.

"Room service." The waitress says.

"I'll get it." Brett leap up from his seat and opens the door. "Thank you." He gives the lady a tip and closes the door again.

"It smells good." I sit up in the chair. "What did you order?"

"Smores." Brett dances with the cart to the sofa. "I have been craving chocolate since the accident."

"Can I help you?" I ask, opening the lid to the warm chocolate and swiping my finger across the top of it brown essence. "Oops, I got some on my leg." I point to the brown spot of chocolate on my inner thigh.

"Let me help you with that." Brett gets on his knees, opens my legs and gently licks the chocolate off my inner thigh, I sigh with desire and hold him there. "Shall I stay here." He breaths on my thigh, the tingles go straight to my core.

"Yes, oh-h." His hands move my legs outward more, lifts me up enough to pull my shorts and panties off. "More, oh-h." The heat from his breath, sends me spiraling and his lip continue kissing until he nears my core. "Brett." I breath out heated.

"Darby." Brett lifts me up into his arms and carries me to the bed. "I want you, but…"

"Let me see you." I nod and slowly he undresses. The scarring is not only on his face, but down his left side to his mid-chest, he stares at me for a response. "I am okay." I pull him closer to my half naked body. "Make love to me, Brett." I help him undress me the rest of the way. His touch sends spasms throughout my body and we orgasm quick.

"I love you, Darby." As his body rolls off mine.

"You want a smore." I laugh.

"I want sa-more of you." He laughs back.

"You're so cute." His lips may not be the same, but they still have the same effect on me, sparks and tingles.

"I need to fly out to Sweden next week." I look at him, sadly. "A special Dermatologist that works only on reconstructive surgeries." "Reviewed my case and thinks she can help me." I feel happy, but sad too. "I want to go see if she can help me."

"Okay, can I go with you?" Brett walks around the bed naked to the bathroom, trying to avoid answering me. "Hey, I asked you a question." Walking into the bathroom behind him.

"Sorry, I can't let you come with me." He states clearly.

"Why?" I stand tall.

"I may be gone for several weeks." He looks at me, his hands are on my shoulders. "You need to get back to work at the spa."

"But, I just got you back." I wrap my arms around his neck. "And the spa been running without me for eight months."

"I understand, really." Brett holds me tight against his chest and we walk back to the bed. "I don't want to be away from you either."

"Wait, you owe me something first." I hold out my left hand, wiggle my ring finger and smile.

"I'll be right back." Brett trots off to his bag sitting in the corner of the bedroom; he walks back over, gets on one knee and pops open the ring box. "Darby Daxton Deel, will you marry me?"

"Yes." I leap into his arms and kiss him. "Oh-h, Brett it is so beautiful." The ring has a one-carat round cut diamond in the middle surrounded by half-carat diamond chips set in fourteen carat white gold band. "I love you."

"I love you, too." We fall back against the floor. "Will you marry me in the Spring?" He smiles.

"I want to marry you today." I kiss his lips with passion. "But in the Spring is fine, too."

"Let's spend the day doing nothing but being naked." Brett snarls sensually. "What do you think?" He picks me up, places me on the bed and lays over me.

"There is no place I'd rather be." I whisper, rolling my body on top of his and taking control; he laughs sweetly. "Except spending the rest of my life with you."

Next week goes by quickly, Brett jets off to Sweden and I am back to work at Allure Me with Abby. It feels weird being at the spa without last year's mayhem going on. After Paige shows me around the Allure's new renovations since I've been away; I found the storage room is efficiently organized, my office has two desks in it now, the special massage table with the water bath is gone too. I've seen the changes, some good and some not so good, but the work flow and clientele's happiness are making the changes worth it. Jimmy and Alexandra introduce me to a handful of our special clientele throughout the next week.

"Alexandra." I smile. "What massage school did you attend?"

"Oh please, call me Alex." Alex smirks. "Mum, is the only one who calls me Alexandra." She stares up at the ceiling. "The school of hard knocks, Miss Darby." I laugh a little.

"U-huh, self-taught." I nod smiling. "Well you have amazing precision." "I like that." I touch her shoulder. "Would you mind if I take your next client?"

"Sure, love to watch a pro." Alex steps back. "Next client is Will Slade." I feel jarred. "Yeah, Brett's brother." Alex tries to smile and hands me a rolled- up towel. "Get to it darlin." I breath deep. "He's in room seven."

"Okay, let's go." I say trying to be confident as I knock on the door. "Will, are you ready?"

"Yes." He says, then silence for a few seconds. "Is that you Darby?" I open the door and smile.

"Yes, Will it's me." He shifts his weight on the table nervously. "Relax." "Remember, massages can only help if you relax."

"I-I don't want to upset, Brett." Will voice shakes. "He'll…"

"Brett is flying to Sweden." I touch his left shoulder. "Relax,

Will." I turn to her. "Alex is only here to observe." "Is that okay?"

"She can participate, if she like." Will utters. "Two for one."

"Not that lucky, roll on you're on your stomach, Will." I laugh, walking to water bath to check the temperature and back to the table. "First, I'll start with stones and then the massage, okay?"

"Yes, sounds nice." He is now relaxing on his stomach. "I'm ready."

"Good." I strategically place the stones down his spine. "Okay, don't move Will." Alex opens the door. "Alex and I will return in about five minutes."

"Mm-mm, yes." Will mumbles. We leave together.

"Alex, you need to finish Will's massage." I announce when we enter the office. "I feel a little dizzy."

"I would, but Will expects you." Alex says with a trouble making tone. "Remember." She crosses her arms against her chest. "Will is a client." "Not Brett's brother." I breath, my eyes wide with raising brows.

"Your right." I take a deep breath. "I am a professional." We walk out of the office to room seven. "Let's do this." I open the door. "Are you ready Will?"

"Oh yeah, relaxed." He says while I remove the stones.

"I am applying hot oils to you, starting at your feet." Alex watches. "If you feel any discomfort let me know."

"U-huh." Will moans out. "I will." Alex smiles, suggesting she wants to laugh out aloud.

Approximately ten minutes into the massage, he starts snoring deeply until I reach his hips and buttocks where his snores turn to sensually moaning. My heart starts racing as I continue my rubbing inward toward his inner thigh, he groans with passion as he lifts his hips up for my hands to slid under to touch his manhood. Instead, I slid my hands back out to his hips and stop, I motion Alex to take over the massage and I leave the room. I stroll quickly back to the office restroom, I splash water on my face and try to catch my breath sitting on the toilet seat. Paige sees me rush to the office and follows quickly behind me.

"Darby, are you okay?" Paige asks from the bathroom doorway.

"No-o." "Yes." I look at her with a fake smile. "I don't know."

"Can I get you a water or coffee?" Paige smiles, she sees that I may start crying. "I think I will get you a cold water." "Be right back." I wave her away.

Paige returns a few seconds later with a water bottle in hand, I take it from her and she leaves me again.

"That was disappointing to see." Alex says to me; twenty minutes later as I stare at my computer screen sitting at my desk. "I thought you were a professional." I look up at her seriously. "Brett would be upset if…"

"No, actually he would be glad I stopped." I stare at her for a reaction, I stand up from my desk. "I do not need to prove myself to you." I walk around my desk to lean on the front of it. "My only concern is why would you want me too." Alex shifts her weight in the doorway and doesn't say a word, only turns and walks away.

"Darby." Paige looks at me from the doorway. "Are you okay." I nod yes. "Good, Abby wants to see you in room ten."

"Okay, thank you Paige." A few minutes later, I walk leisurely to room ten, the hot tub room and open the door, quickly closing it behind me. "Abby, where are you?" I look around the room, the walls where repainted and the window is tinted.

"Down here, Darby." I see her in the hot tub. "Why don't you join me?" I smile, remembering the first time. I nod and go behind the tri-fold to disrobe.

"Ah-h, the water feels nice." I say sliding in the tub naked. "I'll push the button to start it." Abby's hand slides over mine and she smiles.

"No, I've got it programmed on a remote." Abby pushes the red button, when she shows me the small black rectangular box placing it back on the table, then she comes in closer to me. "Are you on a remote too?" Abby gently whispers in my ear. "Because I want to turn you on." She kisses my cheek, caressing my breast with one hand and the other ventures to my lady's garden. "Do you want more?"

"Yes." I kiss her fully on the lips and return the touching favor. "U-huh." Abby breaths heavily in my ear and fingers her probe deeper into my liquid heat.

"Oo-huh." She sighs. "More Darby." We continue sexually taunting each other's lady's gardens until we orgasm together. We kiss again and get out of the hot tub to dress. "See." Abby smiles coming out from behind her tri-fold. "You're a natural."

"You don't feel like, we are cheating on the guys." Abby stares at me concerned and walks over to me.

"No." "I don't." She states clearly. "I love Otis and you love Brett." Abby starts to walk away and stops.

"We enjoy being ourselves, this is only for fun." I nod and smile. "Stop trying to over think it." Abby leaves me in room ten, I turn off the tub and collect the towels for the laundry.

The rest of the day goes by steady, I complete massages for two of our special clientele and they leave extremely satisfied. After running a load of towels through the washer and into the dryer, I find Paige, Alex, Jimmy and Abby standing at the front desk. As I walk towards them, they start clapping harmoniously; I stare at them a little confused.

"Okay, what's going on?" I ask sharply.

“You did great today, a little slow at first.” Alex says aloud. “But an amazing finish.” Abby, Paige and Jimmy are smiling.

“Darby, Mr. Eagleton is one of the hardest people to please.” Abby dances around and hugs me. “And he complemented you, all the way out the door.”

“Really?” I beam. “He didn’t mention anything.”

“Yes, he scheduled with you for the rest of his stay at the hotel.” Abby sputters. “And Queen Bee is also scheduled with you for the rest of her stay too.”

“Oh, wow.” “Thank you, guys.” I laugh a little. “But I am starving and tired, let’s close and go the hotel for dinner.”

“Great idea.” Paige purges. “I’ll get the computer shutdown.”

“I’ll call Otis to get a table ready for us in the Dining Room.” Abby replies, I nod.

“Alex and Jimmy, make sure the rooms are ready for tomorrow.” I direct. “Paige make sure the coffee pot is off.” I walk into the office to turn off my computer and the lights. A few minutes later, we are all out the door heading to the hotel next door.

“Hello, Mrs. Bosworth.” The maître d’ speaks, Abby blushes. “We have your table ready, please follow me.” The group follows behind him to our table.

“It still feels funny.” Abby whispers to me. “When someone calls me Mrs. Bosworth.”

“If would please.” He motions us to sit. “Menus.” We nod. “Very well, I shall return.”

“Abby darling.” Otis says coming up behind her and swing her around to kiss him. “How are you my love?” She kisses him back.

“Honey, hold off on the swinging.” She whispers in his ear. “You’ll make me feel sick to my stomach.” Otis touches his wife’s tummy and smiles. “I love you.” He pulls out her chair for her to sit, pushes her in to the table and takes the seat next to her. “Thank you.” The maître d’ returns with menus and we order.

"Maurice, will take you beverage orders." The maître d' states. "And your food will be out shortly."

Once the food and beverages arrive the conversations continue as we eat and drink; my cellphone rings, it is Brett and I excuse myself from the table.

"Hey Brett, how are you?" I say from the balcony overlooking the Gardens outside.

"It is going to take longer than expected." Brett is ruffled. "But I did the first surgery this morning and it went well." I feel a pang of sadness in my chest.

"I miss you so much, Darby." I hear the loneliness in his voice.

"I can come there, all you have do is say yes." I plead. "I want to be with you."

"I know, but you need to stay busy and not worry about me." Brett's trying to convince himself, this is the right thing to do.

"I love you." I try to be strong. "And worrying about you comes with the territory."

"I love you, too." His voice shrills. "I have to go, I'll call you tomorrow." I can feel him trying to push me away.

"Okay, sleep well." "I love you, Brett."

"Good night, Darby." His call disconnects. I stand looking out into the darkness, until Abby comes outside, and she hugs me.

"Was it Brett?" I nod. She can see the heartbreak on my face. "It is going to be okay." Abby fingers caress my cheek. "We love you." I smile, and we return to the table together.

"Thank you for joining me for dinner." I add. "I am going to my room for some much-needed rest."

After all the time Brett and I spent apart in the last year, and I've climb into to a cold bed, alone; you would think that I would be used to it by now, but it is still torcher. I lay here think about what he'd said, and he was right I need to be busy. First thing tomorrow, I will call the insurance company about my house; Brett mentioned something about rebuilding our home together, maybe I could look at some plans and use the money from my house to get it started. I'll tell Brett tomorrow when he calls, I relax and finally fall asleep.

In the morning, I wake to sunlight in my face and a fresh breeze on my skin; I feel groggy like I had been drugged, when I sit up I am not in my hotel room bed, I'm in a small room in a wooden cabin somewhere not Big Bay Lake. My heart races with fear, when I hear unfamiliar voices outside the door; I get out of bed slowly to check my footing and look out the window. I recognize the lake outside it is Big Buck, the cabin is across from my parents' old cabin near the old hotel. Wilhelm Patrova must be the one behind who took me; the smell of food cooking makes my stomach growl with hunger, I hear a key in the lock of the door and someone will be entering my room soon. I quickly slip back under the covers of the bed, laying still until the person comes in and leaves.

"Miss, please wake up." The young girl says. "You must eat." She touches my arm. "Please, I'll get into trouble." I roll over to see what appears to be a teenager with short blonde hair and a crooked smile. "Thank you." She smiles, showing only three teeth in the top of her mouth. "It is good food, I made it myself." The girl takes a spoonful and eats it. "See, it is good."

"Okay." I take the plate of food and spoon from the girl. "Thank you." "What's your name?"

"Daniella Patrova." She smiles. "I am Wilhelm's granddaughter." She adds. "And Nicola's daughter." Daniella's head drops down. "He's dead."

"I am so sorry." I touch her hand and she pulls it away fast. "I never knew him." She nods, starts to leave the room. "How long have I been here?"

"A few days." "I will be back for the dishes." Daniella shuts the door behind her. "Soon."

After scoffing the food down quickly and swallowing the glass of vodka; I return to the window to look out, I see no armed guards walking around outside the cabin. The idea of escaping sounds good to me, but before I can climb out the window Daniella opens the door; she stares at me surprised and shuts the door behind her quietly.

"Don't try to leave here." Daniella speaks softly. "I can't help you if you do." I stare at her questioningly.

"What?" "I don't understand." Daniella takes two steps closer to me, she is by my side. "Why?"

"I am a prisoner in my own home." She whispers. "My grandfather is a criminal and a murderer." "I know who blew up Mr. Slade's mansion." She has my interest. "And he knows I know."

"Oh-h no." I touch her hand. "I need to get away from here." "Daniella, please."

"Yes, I do too." Daniella adds. "When my grandfather and his men leave." She walks towards the door. "I'll be back to get you." "Okay." I nod, and she leaves the room, locking the door after she shuts it.

A few hours later, in the quiet air I hear the door lock click; I wait to see if someone enters the room before I try to open the door, no one comes inside the room. Nervously, I open the door slowly, poking my head beyond the opening to see if Daniella is there; the hallway is empty and an eerie feeling creeps over me, I know there is something wrong, but I leave the room cautiously anyway. I take seven steps to the left of the room doorway and I hear voices at the end of the hallway coming from the stairwell, so I stop to listen. Daniella is arguing with someone about me.

"Dzya-doo-lya(grandpa), she doesn't belong here." Daniella's voices. "Neither, do I."

"Sorry, my darling." An older man grumbles. "Brett Slade has to pay for your father's death."

"He didn't kill my father." She declares. "My Dzya-dzen-ka(Uncle) did." Then a loud slapping noise and Daniella cries out loud.

"Don't say such things about your Uncle." He hollers, she still crying. I walk slowly to the top of the stairs.

"Mr. Patrova!" His arm is up for another swing to slap Daniella again. "Stop!" He stares up to the top of the stairwell. "It isn't her fault."

"Daniella, you let her out." Wilhelm glares at his granddaughter. "Why?"

"Darby doesn't belong here." Daniella says looking at me, as I walk slowly down the stairs. "Let her go!"

"You disobey me." Patrova throws his hands up in the air. "Tarnish, your father's memory."

"No Dzya-doo-lya." She smiles at him. "He would be proud of me." Wilhem looks down at the floor.

"Mr. Patrova, may I ask you something?" I say at the bottom of the stairwell, and Wilhelm looks up at me. "Why are you trying to hurt Mr. Slade?" "What did he do?"

“Mr. Slade destroyed a very important relationship with a very lucrative investor.” Wilhelm belts out. “He costs me a lot of money every day now.”

“Oh, so it is a money issue.” I give him a disturb look. “Not as if he killed someone.” “Your absurd, Mr. Patrova.”

“What do you mean young lady?” He stands, hands on his hip glaring at me.

“You take a life, as it is nothing to you.” “Did you even love your own children?” I breath. “Or are they just a bargaining chip to you?”

“What?” Wilhelm reaches for his gun in its holster. “I should shoot you and make you the example.”

“What if I broker a deal between you and Mr. Slade?” I smile. “He trusts me, not you.”

“Deal?” His forehead wrinkles. “What do you have in mind?”

“The investor that needs to be re-assured.” Wilhelm's forehead relaxes. “Who is it?” I ask.

“Diego Fortuna, Italian Ministry Procurer.” He says interested. “It is very difficult to get to him.”

“I think Mr. Slade can handle it.” I stand ready. “He is…very good at taking care of business.” Wilhelm smiles and nods in agreement.

“Okay, you may leave here.” He points his index finger at me. “But you better deliver, understand.”

“Yes, Mr. Patrova.” I sigh “I understand.”

“Let's go, Darby.” Daniella expels, taking my hand. “Before he changes his mind.” We hurry quickly out the front door of the old hotel and through the woods.

“My family's old cabin is not far.” I smile, pointing to the other side of lake. “It is right over there.”

“No, I have a car stashed in the woods.” Daniella replies. “Follow me.” A few minutes later, we are next to an old grey sedan. “The keys are under the visor on the driver's side." I climb inside the vehicle and start the engine. Daniella follows my lead.

"Where are we going?" I ask looking at the teenager seated next to me.

"To find Mr. Slade." She stares at me. "You know where he is, right?"

"Yes." I drive the car out of the woods slowly. "He is out of the country." "But, I think I can contact him."

"Let's hope so." Daniella stares out of the front window. "My grandfather will be very upset."

We drive the rest of the way to the Big Bay Lake Hotel in silence; when we arrive, I leave her in the lobby with Abby to speak to Otis.

"Hello Otis." I say when I enter his office, he turns slowly and smiles surprised.

"Darby, what happened to you?" Otis fumbles with his coffee cup.

"Wilhelm Patrova took me to the old hotel at Big Buck Lake." His forehead frowns. "He wants Brett, not me." I add. "But, I struck a deal with him."

"You did?" Otis looks concerned, when I sit in the chair in the front of his desk. "For what?"

"He wants Brett to fix the relationship between Diego Fortuna and himself." His fingers begin tapping on the desktop. "I guess Wilhelm thinks it was Brett's fault it was broken."

"It was and is Brett's fault." Otis retorts. "Diego is a bastard." He shifts his body in his chair. "His idea is to screw everyone out of money." I sit up and listen intently. "So, Brett stole his outside dealings from Patrova and made it look like Diego did it to him." Relaxing, I sit back against the chair.

"Wow, that's why he blames Brett for the broken relationship." I smile. "Even though he saved Patrova from getting screwed out of money." I utter. "Has Brett called you since he left?"

"No." "But, he called Abby when you went missing." My heart is hammering in my chest.

"Is he okay?" I swallow hard. "Was he upset?"

"You need to ask Abby." He stands up from his desk and walks around to me, I stand up and he hugs me. "I am glad you're okay."

"Thank you." I smile. "We need to thank Daniella. Patrova's granddaughter." "She saved me."

"Daniella." Otis face frowns. "Granddaughter?" His face goes pale, staring into space. "Oh, shit." Otis walks back around his desk and plops down into his chair. "She is Fortuna's granddaughter too."

"What?" I spill. "Who's?" My mouth goes dry. "Daniella is both their bargaining chips." Otis nods. "We need to keep her safe."

"I'll call downstairs, have them sent up here." I walk around the chair, standing behind it. "You'll need to meet them at the elevator and bring them in here." I nod, and he dials the front desk, speaks quickly and hangs up the phone. "Go now, I'll call security."

I leave his office to wait by the elevator. It dawns on me waiting for the elevator to arrive, Otis has been acting a little different since he recognized Daniella as Fortuna's granddaughter as well. I wonder if Brett was even involved in the Fortuna/Patrova deal? The elevator is taking too long to come up; so, I use the phone next to the doors and call the front desk. The attendant tells me Otis never call him and the ladies are still sitting in the lobby.

"Max, don't let them leave with anyone." I push the button to the elevator. "I'll be there in a few minutes.

"Yes Ma'am." His voice stops for a second. "Even Mr. Bosworth."

"Yes, especially Mr. Bosworth." I voice shrills. "Stall him, I am on the way down now."

"Yes Ma'am." We hang up the phones at the same time. Max sees Mr. Bosworth hug his wife after he exits his private elevator. "Mr. Bosworth." Max says aloud. "Excuse me, Sir." Otis sees the young man waving as he walks toward them.

"Yes, Max." Otis looks at him sternly. "What wrong?" He places his hands on his hips. "What is it?"

"Otis don't be so gruff." Abby staring at him with a frown.

"Sir, sorry to bother you." Max takes a quick breath. "But, Darren in Maintenance needs you to sign-off on his parts order, today."

"This can't wait?" Otis is upset.

"No, Sir." Max states nervously. "If he doesn't send the order by noon today, it will be another two weeks before we receive them."

"Okay-okay." Otis takes his wife's hand kisses the top of it. "Call Darren, have the order ready for my signature." He huffs. "Sorry, darling duty calls." Otis walks away fast, as the elevator door opens, and I step out.

"Abby." I walk up to them. "Daniella." "Follow me, quickly." We walk outside the hotel to the Spa and enter through the basement door.

"Darby, what's going on?" Abby asks staring at me, while tugging the sleeve of my shirt and I stop at the stairs. Abby releases me.

"Ask Daniella." I look at her and she gives a snide smile. "She's the one with all the stories." "Right, Daniella?"

"So, Darby." "You've got it figured out?" Daniella grabs Abby's arm. "I am the evil granddaughter." She snickers. "Of Diego and Wilhelm." Abby sucks in a gasp loudly and struggles in Daniella's grip. "Don't worry, nothing will happen to you." "As long as Otis and Brett return on their investment." Abby stare at each other confused.

"What investment?" I inquire, suspiciously.

"Yeah, what investment.?" Abby adds.

"Tis-tis." Daniella waves a free hand in the air. "Never you mind." "Darby, call Brett."

"He's out of the country." Daniella's nose wrinkles and her eyes glare at me as I reply. "Having surgery."

"Try him anyway!" She screams gruffly. "Or Otis won't have a wife and child to come home to." Abby's eyes glare, either from anger or fear or both.

"Okay, I'll try." I carefully take the cellphone handed to me. "I hope he answers." I dial his number and the line is ringing. Brett's voicemail clicks on. "Brett, call me as soon as possible." I breath. "It is very important." I stop the call and hand Daniella her phone. "I tried." I say nervously.

"For all your sakes." Daniella spouts viscously. "He…"

"I know…he will call me." I stop her, feeling a cold chill go up my spine. "I know it." We climb the stairs to my office. "My phone is in my desk." I sigh. "I'll check it for messages." I sit behind my desk in my chair, opening the top drawer below to retrieve my phone; while Abby and Daniella sit in the chairs in front of my desk, staring at me intensely. "No, messages…yet."

"Try him again." Daniella persists. "Until he answers."

"Ok…I will." I dial Brett's number and wait for it to connect. "Hello, Brett." I hear crackling on the line. "Are you there?" A voice speaks, but I can't tell if it is Brett from the interference on the line. "Brett, if it is you, call me back." I disconnect and wait for my phone to ring, but it doesn't right away.

"Darby, what's wrong?" Abby stands up, walking around to the back of the chair. "Was it him?"

"I couldn't make out the voice." Staring at her, then Daniella. "I hope it was." My phone rings and I answer it quickly. "Hello." A man's voice speaks and nod. "I understand." I frown. "Yes, I will." "Thanks."

"Was it Brett?" Daniella's eye sparkle.

"No, it was his surgeon." "She said that Brett has undergone three of his six surgeries." I utter guarded. "Right now, he is in recovery." "And he won't be able to call me back until later today."

"Well, Daniella are going to wait to kill me or not?" Abby adds sarcastically, then turns to me. "And why did his surgeon call you back?"

"I was surprised too." I sigh. "Brett told her, if she saw my number or name show up on his phone." Abby stares curiously at me. "She was to call me back and give me an update on his condition."

"A voice recognition software." Daniella says searing. "It is a rich man's game." She tugs on Abby's arm. "Call your husband, now."

"Okay." Abby's struggles to get her phone out of back pocket of her skinny jeans. "This would be a lot easier, if you would let go of my arm." Daniella loosens her hold. "I am pregnant, it is a little tighter than usual." "Thank you." Abby calls Otis and Daniella sits next to her, very close. "Eaves drop much." "Otis, honey." Daniella's face frowns and grabs the phone from Abby.

"Yes, darling Otis." "This Daniella Patrova." She stands and walks around the back of the chairs in front of my desk. "I want you and Brett to fix the disaster with the Italians." Daniella runs her skinny fingers through Abby's hair. "Or your wife and child will pay." She disconnects the call and tosses the phone on Abby's lap. Abby stares at me, scared. "I think I may have gotten his attention." Daniella tugs Abby up from her chair by the arm. "Let's go ladies."

Meanwhile back at the Big Bay Hotel, Otis is racing around his office like a mad man trying to find his old phonebook with Reggie Delano's number in it, Diego's right-hand man. The number rings several times, finally the call connects, and the man speaks. "Reggie."

Now, Daniella leads us back outside the Allure Me Spa, where there is a long black stretch limo waiting for us; Abby and I enter the vehicle not knowing what the outcome will be, Daniella tells the limo driver to take us to the airport. We arrive at the private runway within an hour; the jet engines are gearing up when we enter the cabin and take our seats. Two armed guards are standing inside the cabin watching us intently.

> "Please do not try to leave this cabin." She announces, while Abby and I stare at her. "Seat belts, please." Daniella turns to walk away from us and looks back. "I am going to talk to the pilot." We look at each other. "Be ready for takeoff."
>
> "Darby, where is she taking us?" Abby's body twitches in her seat. "I am worried."
>
> "I know, I am scared too." Abby's eyes tear up as my lips shimmy. "Otis fix this."
>
> "U-huh, I hope soon." Abby adds buckling her seat belt. We can feel the jet rolling back out of park into the runway, as the jet sets for takeoff. "Daniella, where are you taking us?" She sits in a seat next to the window across from us.
>
> "Oh, sorry ladies it is on a need to know basis." Daniella smirks. "And you don't need to know."

The jet engines roar, it moves quickly down the runway and we enter air space. I notice an unfamiliar smell in the cabin, start feeling very sleepy, my vision is blurry; I can hardly see Daniella, it looks like she is wearing a mask, and I pass out. Unfortunately, what happens next is…

TO BE CONTINUED…

PAGETURNER
PRESS&MEDIA

CPSIA information can be obtained
at www.ICGtesting.com
Printed in the USA
LVHW040529200122
708837LV00002B/94